Praise for *Playing with Wildfire*

"An immersive story of a changing landscape, innovatively told."

—*KIRKUS REVIEWS*

"Pritchett's creativity is boundless as she bends formats and blends voices in this vibrant paean to nature's fragility. At levels both micro and macro, Pritchett brings an electric connectivity to her portrait of the precariousness of this one wild, threatened world."

—*BOOKLIST*, starred review

"Fierce, vivid, and closely observed, *Playing with Wildfire* is an exercise in paying attention. And if 'attention is the most basic form of love,' the earth is not the only thing in danger. Love is an endangered ecology too, and there is an inherent mutualism to what's required for healing."

—*FOREWORD REVIEWS*, starred review

"Pritchett's novel is wise and attentive. The broad sweeping compassion of this polyvocal novel takes my breath away. These many modes of seeing and understanding are the realities from which we weave the story of the world."

—CAMILLE T. DUNGY, *Soil: The Story of a Black Mother's Garden*

"In *Playing with Wildfire*, Laura Pritchett writes with characteristic intelligence and humor. Her worldview in these burning times is a rare cocktail, passion and wisdom in equal parts, administered here with refreshing innovation."

—RICK BASS, *For a Little While*

"Inventive, sassy, urgent. *Playing with Wildfire* is rich with surprises of all kinds, from start to finish."

—ALYS(

"In this gorgeous pyrobiographic novel, we see the fire in everything it touches: the deer, the house, the lungs, the heart. The form of this novel, like fire itself, mutates and shifts as it moves through, offering up glimmers of dreams and truth within the ruin. In this generative work on the ravages of climate change, Laura Pritchett gives us what we most urgently need: a way to stay with it."

—BETH PIATOTE, *The Beadworkers: Stories*

"*Playing with Wildfire* is a wise and imaginative collection in which aspen trees sing warnings, moose and raven describe a terrifying inferno, and Mother Earth sends urgent postcards to humanity. Pritchett's expansive exploration of what community means in the face of climate change fueled megafires includes a cast of endearing and original characters who split apart and come together and find ways to keep living joyfully."

—CLAIRE BOYLES, *Site Fidelity*

"Incendiary, evocative writing that crackles on the page. Pritchett paints a complete and tender picture of one small community's reckoning with the worst wildfire in Colorado history."

—MOLLY IMBER, Maria's Bookshop

"Celebrated nature writer Laura Pritchett takes the reader on a journey that is at once singular and daring, intimate and illuminating. *Playing with Wildfire* is a must-read for all of us enduring unprecedented wildfires as well as anyone who wants to experience the possibilities of brilliant storytelling."

—CMARIE FUHRMAN, *Camped Beneath the Dam: Poems* and co-editor of *Native Voices*

"For those of us who live in the West, wildfire is no longer a distant threat but a regular companion. *Playing with Wildfire* captures this reality by embracing the whole of life in the Anthropocene—music, food, sex, illness, hope, motherhood, addiction, work, and more—in stories as breathtakingly true and tender as they are, yes, playful."

—ANA MARIA SPAGNA, *Pushed: Miners, a Merchant, and (Maybe) a Massacre*

Praise for *The Blue Hour*

"A pitch-perfect story from a superb writer."

—*Library Journal*, starred review

"Within this close-knit community, Pritchett wondrously binds the core of humanity to these stories of incandescent characters. A richly sensual, tenderly proffered portrait of the most vulnerable yet appealing aspects of the human condition."

—*BOOKLIST*, starred review

"Graced with characters so alive, so full of quirky humanity, you miss them when you've finished the book,and written in prose as clear and gorgeous as a mountain afternoon, *The Blue Hour* isn't just about the many ways love can end—it's about how connection jumpstarts when you least expect it, too."

—CAROLINE LEAVITT, author of *Cruel Beautiful World*

"Laura Pritchett's exquisitely-linked novel of short stories manages to be all at once poetic and funny, heart-breaking and true. And the role of sex as social bonder, marriage breaker is so beautifully addressed. This is a snapshot of the new West, as seen from that most breathtaking perspective—the inside out."

—ALEXANDRA FULLER, author of *Leaving Before the Rains*

"The terrifically talented Laura Pritchett has written an immersive, sexy, singular novel. Each of its characters are beautifully drawn and infused with desire and sadness and joy. This is the kind of book I am always looking for and am very grateful to have found in the lyrical and heartbreaking pages of *The Blue Hour*."

—CHRISTINE SNEED, author of *Paris, He Said*

"In this place charged with dusk, still held by light, *The Blue Hour* sets lightning on the sky."

—SHANN RAY, author of *American Copper*

Playing with Wildfire

playing
with
(*wild*)fire

A Novel

Laura Pritchett

TORREY HOUSE PRESS

Salt Lake City • Torrey

First Torrey House Press Edition, February 2024

Published by Torrey House Press
Salt Lake City, Utah
www.torreyhouse.org

International Standard Book Number: 978-1-948814-89-8
E-book ISBN: 978-1-948814-90-4
Library of Congress Control Number: 2022951330

Cover design by Kathleen Metcalf
Interior design by Gray Buck-Cockayne
Distributed to the trade by Consortium Book Sales and Distribution

Torrey House Press offices in Salt Lake City sit on the homelands of
Ute, Goshute, Shoshone, and Paiute nations. Offices in Torrey are on the
homelands of Southern Paiute, Ute, and Navajo nations.

To those who have seen the sun go red and the sky darken. To experts who extended a helping hand, whether tired-eyed at a desk or covered in soot. To those in the public eye, and to those unseen and unsung. To the general populace who fed, coordinated, and sheltered animals and people. To those in the future who will do the same. To those who have died by wildfire, including from illnesses from toxic air. To bear and moose and deer and our flying companions. To kids raising funds with lemonade stands. To our sky holding billowing smoke. To our planet laboring to heal.

Contents

"Unusual events being necessarily limited in number, it is but natural that these should be excavated over and over in the hope of discovering a yet undiscovered vein."

—Amitav Ghosh, *The Great Derangement*

"If you're lucky, a place will shape and cut and bend you, will strengthen and weaken you. You trade your life for the privilege of this experience—the joy of a place, the joy of blood family; the joy of knowledge gotten by listening and observing."

—Rick Bass, *The Sky, The Stars, The Wilderness*

"Summer on the high plateau can be delectable as honey; it can also be a roaring scourge. To those who love a place, both are good, since both are part of its essential nature. And it is to know its essential nature that I am seeking here."

—Nan Shepherd, *The Living Mountain*

"We may not have wings or leaves, but we humans do have words. Language is our gift and our responsibility. I've come to think of writing as an act of reciprocity with the living land. Words to remember old stories, words to tell new ones, stories that bring science and spirit back together."

—Robin Wall Kimmerer, *Braiding Sweetgrass*

Deer in the poppies

GRETEL

FOR THE LOVE. FOR THE LOVE OF ALL THAT'S HOLY, JUST *pretend it's foggy Ireland*, Gretel told herself, but no, it was ashy Colorado, and the valley was socked in with wildfire smoke, and the sky was orange-gray, brown-gray, Grey Poupon-gray, and it was disgusting and no use pretending otherwise. It was disgusting and it was not Ireland. Even her imagination had limits.

Burned pine needles—still in the shape of pine needles—were currently littering her new deck just outside the bedroom's sliding glass doors. She watched from bed and said *pretty damn grim* aloud to the afternoon sun, an orb of red so shrouded by the plume that staring didn't hurt her eyes at all.

Her plan had been to spend the day tacking chicken wire underneath the new deck, perhaps with the neighbor kid, Alexis. The point was to prevent future catastrophes, such as skunks moving in, but what was the point of that? So she stayed in bed and when she awoke next it was still shitty, except the sun was lower, closer to the mountains. The bright blue birdbath was filled with black water and the sunflowers blooming next to it—volunteers from the birdfeeder—stood in defiance to the ash. So did the finch, clinging to the sunflower upside-down, though the dead one below clarified that defiance had its limits. There were some bright red poppies too, the only flowers to bloom after she'd cast a huge number of wildflower seeds, the others chomped down by deer.

She fell asleep again and woke again. Ever since she'd had COVID, she slept like this, in fragments. She saw now that a deer was in the poppies. The doe wasn't eating them, poppies being toxic to deer, or so she'd heard, but standing *in* them and eating the lilacs. This was the same deer that she'd tried to chase out of her yard all summer—this doe was young and small, not the mother of the twins, and the only one likely to jump the fence despite Gretel having put up a higher wire. Since the fire, she'd taken to plinking the deer on the butt with the BB gun, which she figured felt like a small finger-flick, given that the distance was so great. Her brothers had shot her with BB guns at a much closer range, and it was never catastrophic, so she supposed she shouldn't feel guilty. Although she did, of course. It was maybe a horrible thing? Still, it was an experiment of sorts, to see if the deer would exhibit some behavioral plasticity and associate her yard with unpleasant mild pains on the ass—just like humans might change their ways after the pain-in-the-ass of wildfires? Like she might become a more energetic person?

She wanted to go back to sleep but her nose started bleeding and she was forced up to get a wad of toilet paper, and while she was up, and after she peed, she picked up the BB gun resting against the wall in the corner, opened the glass door, and said, *Scram, lady. All I want are my shitfuck lilacs* and plinked the deer.

The deer flicked her ears and turned around to look at her but did not move. The doe had plenty of other land to munch on—the house was surrounded by an enormous expanse of pastureland and foothills—sure, not lilacs, but still. So she plinked again but missed; the deer didn't move but the lilac branch above it did. She supposed she wanted the deer to feel shitty, because she felt shitty, and because she wanted just one thing to remain safe and alive. So she stepped outside the door to yell louder, and at the sight of her, the deer jumped and bounded over the fence and onto the county road.

Then she heard the screech and thud. Her first thought was: *Are you serious?*

Her second thought: *Actually, I knew that might happen.*

She walked outside and turned the corner of the house to

see an old rust-red truck, the same color as her pajamas. She thought for a moment about the happenstance of that, too. An older and smaller and no doubt wiser woman, someone who wouldn't have plinked or yelled at a deer, was swinging herself out of the truck and moving toward the prone deer. She approached the woman and said, "You okay? Want me to call the sheriff?" but the woman shook her head, *no*, and Gretel understood that the woman was likely one of the workers from the farm over by the dairy, over-worked and under-paid and definitely wanting to stay off the radar of the sheriff.

"I'm sorry, I'm so sorry," Gretel said, and indeed it felt like a river rock was stuck in her throat. Now she felt worse. She was a disgusting human being, as disgusting as the sky, and she had just made this woman's day disgusting. And the deer—how much more disgusting could it get? Than unnecessary death? They stood side-by-side and stared at the deer, which looked fine but was clearly dented on the inside, and then at the truck, which was visibly dented but drivable.

"Do you want to call an insurance company? The sheriff?" she said again.

"No," the woman said. "No. He's not…"

"I know. I'm sorry."

They sighed and stood in silence.

"I'll give you money to fix it."

"Okay," the woman said. "But it wasn't your fault."

"It was."

The woman quirked an eyebrow at her, but she didn't explain, and so they both took a step toward the deer, who now had blood streaming out of her nose. Gretel picked up a warm hind leg and the woman picked up the other and together with a *one, two, three,* they lurched the deer forward. The deer was warm and heavy, but it wasn't far, and the other woman was very strong; otherwise, it simply wouldn't have been possible. It very nearly wasn't. Gretel was huffing from the effort, and from the ash, and she was surprised for a moment that she wasn't shy about the pajamas, stained from period blood on the butt—while her sleep was now fragmented, her blood flow was nearly constant since COVID. She felt a glimmer of curiosity about her brain being in such a fog. She also felt something akin to stunned awe: she had wondered if this would happen, and then it did. Simple as that. Perhaps humans predicted possibilities all the time and yet did not change their behavior, and that seemed odd.

By the time she'd jogged inside to rifle through her drawers for some cash and come back out, the red truck was gone in the twilight. She climbed back into bed. She stared at the red poppies and the yellow sunflowers and the blue birdbath filled with black water and the white ash falling like snowflakes. *Pretend it's Christmas Eve and it's snowing,* she told herself, but no, imagination had its limits. She shouldn't have scared the deer. She should be more grateful for this community and take better care of its inhabitants. Also, she probably had until tomorrow to pack her go-bag for potential mandatory evacuations, and for the deer to start smelling, which meant she had until then to get it together.

LOU

The sky was getting crazier by the minute. Lou figured it was probably the most wondrous sky he'd ever seen, in fact, so changeable in hue, just like the stock trailers going up the canyon were all sorts of colors, all sorts of models and makes and years, all sorts of levels of dented, and between the vehicles and the sky, he felt like a circus was going on in his eyes. It made him woozy.

The evacuation center for large animals was at the elementary school parking lot and the call had been put out on the radio and social media: anyone with trailers was supposed to help out. It struck him as strange, how despite the enormous technology and too-big government, it still came down to a semi-disorganized mess of regular people guided by a volunteer posse which mainly consisted of his neighbor, Autumn, on her phone at her kitchen table, and whomever she could pester.

He wasn't able to help with the animals, though, because he didn't have a stock trailer. Instead, he was driving Autumn's new Tacoma to hitch up the nice motorboat of a friend of Autumn's to get it off the mountain, the friend being busy evacuating other items. The fire had been going for weeks, maybe a solid month, but it had just flared up in the heat and wind—had gone from thirty thousand acres to sixty thousand acres yesterday, and from sixty thousand to a hundred thousand today.

At the mouth of the canyon, he braked and glanced right, since this last intersecting county road was dangerous. You couldn't count on the cross-traffic to heed the stop sign; he'd seen a wreck or two there. And strangely—wasn't it weird how the world worked like this sometimes?—in the exact moment he glanced, he saw an old pickup collide with a deer.

His foot hit the brake by instinct, and a jolt of *oh shit* zipped up his spine. But he kept driving. Literally, there was nothing he could do—this was a narrow road with no turnarounds and the red truck was now out of sight because he'd rounded a curve and now would round many more curves before he got to a boat in the mountains. *Fuckin-A that was shitty, poor dude and poor deer and I didn't realize the apocalypse would feel so heavy.*

PAIGE

Paige heard a distant but distinct thud while she put the chickens in the back of her car—Bok-lava, Oh-Beetle-Beetle, Henrietta, Fred. *That sucks for someone,* she thought as she thrust the last chicken in the car and turned around to go inside for her whole CPU—it was ancient and big and heavy and yet contained so much important stuff which, of course, she'd failed to back up. She could only hope the chickens didn't shit on it, and also, that someday in the future, she'd learn to be more organized and prepared, have her life together. Most other people seemed to manage this and she wasn't sure why it should be any different for her, it's not like she had a brain defect. Sure, at the moment, she was too high—edibles were hard to gauge and unpredictable—and besides, her eyes and lungs itched and it made it hard for the brain to work correctly, it was *fog fog fog* up there in that skull of hers, but eventually, she hoped, she would be better able to cope with life's variations. How to be *proactive* and *look ahead*—that was the battle of her life. And the battle of humanity as well. One at which they were most obviously failing. Which caused her brain to fail even more. A negative feedback loop if ever there was one.

The chickens were bokking and fluttering all over and she put out her arm to keep them in the back seat, away from her duffle bag and box of documents, and she drove past the small cluster of homes that constituted her neighborhood: two trailers, one cabin, two hippie A-frames. Most had warring yard signage, a new development of these past bifurcated years. She turned on the main road heading down the canyon. The hotels in town were all booked, she'd heard, as a result of people fleeing the mountain. She supposed she'd stop by Naomi's house at the base of the canyon and offer free babysitting for that cute little Medusa-haired kid whose name she forgot but who was always playing with toy horses, and she'd be welcome to stay because Naomi had her hands full and extra bedrooms and a kind heart.

Halfway to town, a white junker car sped by her, going 100 at least, passed her on a curve, scaring the shit out of her. It was her fucker neighbor, and at least she had life down better than that guy, because at least she was living a life that didn't put other people in direct and obvious danger. But still, she wondered if there would be a future point in time when she could look at her life and think, *Ah-ha! I know where my flash drives are, I am kicking ass, I am grown up and managing life.*

SHERM

The deer was still warm and why not? It looked like a clean snap at the neck. Sherm stood considering it in the tall roadside grass.

Pros: income from bartending at the saloon was gone because of 'Rona, and sure, he'd need more food this winter and the community food cabinet felt embarrassing, plus, he had space in his freezer, and plus, it would be putting the death to use.

Cons: he was in a salty, pissy mood already. And it's just that he'd never eaten roadkill before, and also, maybe eating roadkill was illegal in Colorado, unlike his home state of Alaska, though in the end, that was a non-issue—who cared about what was legal anymore?

It would be easier to gut her roadside but he just wanted to be away from people, all people, he hated people, and this intersection was dangerous and currently busy (for a county road) because of the fire, so he improvised a ramp out of boards already in the truck bed (he'd intended to take them to the dump, one less flammable pile of junk around, but he'd been too tired). He also had some rope and bungee cords buried on the floorboard and was able to rig up a system and haul her up, bit by bit. Luckily, she wasn't large, which made a one-man show possible, though it wasn't easy and had him wheezing. People didn't really know how hard it is to move a dead deer, or a dead anything, and it occurred to him that was why he was always so tired, COVID-longhauler for sure. He was tired of moving his dead lonely soul and sick body around. He was heavy to himself.

He heaved her body into his truck bed and stood panting, running through the progression of things he'd do next. He was having trouble thinking through things and it helped to tap his head with each agenda item. He'd:

–get her home,

–hoist her by the back legs to the lower rafter of the tree fort left by some long-ago renter,

—skin her, gut her,

—dump all the junk into an old plastic bin,

—then dump all that far from the house so as not to attract that bear,

—butcher her.

He'd need to do it all right away because it was late August and warm. He didn't have butcher paper—he hadn't been planning on this—but he'd improvise with something. Or maybe his neighbors, Mariana or Paige, had some, and regardless, he'd share the meat with them (but not the jackass with the white car).

He hurried, though the sheriff was busy with doing real work for a change, and regardless, getting a deer off the road was a help to society. But he felt he had to move fast because he didn't want to deal with another human, and also, if he didn't go fast, it wouldn't get done at all. He glanced to the side as he pulled himself up into the cab and noticed a woman looking out from the chinked log cabin at the corner. She was standing in front of a glass door that opened onto a porch and was mostly secluded by trees and lilacs—he wouldn't have seen her save for the red pajamas she was wearing and the yellow sunflowers near her door. Color and movement were what caught the eye.

She offered a little wave, and he imagined she meant, *thank you, hang in there, I'm sorry we're all feeling so shitty,* and for the first time in so long, he smiled. He had the sudden prediction that he'd be very grateful for the meat this winter, and that each time he ate some, he'd think of a red-pajamaed woman.

ALEXIS

Holy-moly. Alexis watched two teenage horse riders trotting by her window while holding her toy horse and she was jealous and also surprised they were riding at all because it was super smoky out today. She wanted a horse, and she also wanted to kiss that teenage boy because she was super-curious about kisses, and she also wanted to set up a lemonade stand.

A man pulled over on the side of the road with a boat. She wished to be on a boat. A boat or a horse. The man got out of his truck to check something about the boat, maybe it wasn't tied to his truck very good, and when he was done, he bent over, put his hands on the boat, and his shoulders moved like maybe he was crying.

She wished she could go outside but her mom had ticked off the reasons on her fingers. No, because of

a) the COVID and

b) the ash and

c) the mountain lion in the neighborhood, which was probably lurking around closer to the homes because of the fire.

So she went back to coloring and didn't know the name for this feeling inside her because it was more than sad and maybe adults knew the name of it, it was more like crackling, like electricity needed to come out, like you needed to run off but there was nowhere to run off to. What was that word she learned? Voltage. What if she couldn't handle the voltage of this and she got fried?

She didn't care if her mom would be mad. She picked up her drawing of the map of the mountain and ran it out to the man.

NORMAN

The rest of the Search and Rescue team was up the canyon but Norman had been assigned to the Sleeping Bear Mountain area and thank god because for the first time in his life, he felt at his limit. Like something might snap or break or shatter, and all he had to do was slowly drive around a little neighborhood trying to find the owner of an abandoned vehicle which might indicate that someone was out hiking and unaware that the fire had moved east so quickly and that person should be rescued and his job was to ask around. Also, he wanted to drive to the very end of Sugar Bear Lane, a dirt road with a few houses clustered together, to see if there was anything to be seen. Help anyone evacuate if needed. Plus, a woman he'd seen at the bar lived in one of these houses, and she'd always struck him as put-together and kind and maybe she needed a friendly hand.

Of the domiciles there, the first had hand-painted plywood signs leaning against the fence, BLACK LIVES MATTER and DEFUND THE POLICE. He wondered if that was her. The second house had put up plywood that read THANK YOU POLICE and SAINT MICHAEL PROTECT OUR POLICE. The third house had a sign that said BE THE REASON SOMEONE SMILES TODAY. The last home, an old cabin, hidden in the woods, had no sign, nothing to say on the matters of the day. He made a U-turn and noticed a guy unloading a dead deer from the back of a truck—odd, since it wasn't hunting season quite yet—but he didn't have the energy to care. He was S&R, not the law, not regulatory agencies, and besides, the neighborhood wasn't under mandatory evacuation yet, just optional, so he had no reason to pester anyone. His job, as he thought of it, was guided by the Standard Firefighting Orders of 1) Be alert. 2) Keep calm. 3) Think clearly. 4) Act decisively, which seemed like a good approach to this whole COVID-wildfire-shit year. He wished he knew where the woman was, if she was safe. If, frankly, he could connect with any kind woman. Maybe that was the whole reason he'd volunteered for the Search and Rescue team in the first place—hoping that somehow, he'd meet a woman by helping her. Even more than sex, he wanted right relations. He wanted to hug the right woman, one who happened to be in need of the right guy, which was him, and together, they'd make things better.

MARIANA

In all her life, this was the first time she'd hit a deer. Of course, Mariana had considered the possibility, since so many gathered by the road, especially at dawn and dusk. It was just math—a numbers game—but she wished she didn't have to drive all these days with the knowledge that eventually she'd hit one, and wished that today had not been the day, this day that tía Maria in California had died of COVID.

It was true, however, that one could not pace the timing of shit.

Also, it was true that you could anticipate something but keep trudging on anyway. As she would. She would drive home, pack up her things, get off the mountain. She would sleep at the dairy—they'd offered her the couch in the break room. Or perhaps she'd visit that woman in the red pajamas, if only because the woman had offered her money and apology in both English and Spanish and in a way that seemed very sincere and very sad, and sometimes you just had to reach out with concision and force and connect with someone.

But first, she had to stop shaking. Hitting the deer was perhaps the last straw for her nervous system. She couldn't stop the shivers. She had to sit down for a minute, and drink tea. She kept saying, *Okay, halt, Shivers. Halt now. Halt. This isn't the last straw. There's always another straw. Tranquila. Tranquila.* But she couldn't move. Instead, she sat there, watching a Search and Rescue truck slowly drive down the street in the smog, pausing to look at her BE THE REASON sign, the one she'd made to get the other two neighbors to shut up.

She wished he would come in and help her.

She wished for lobos. To keep down the deer. To make the world balanced again.

She wished for the deer to have its life back.

She wished for the rains to come.

She wished for the planet to be healthy and strong.

She wished for the lack of foreknowledge.

She wished that everyone felt less fragmented, less alone.

She wished the fire wasn't growing but it was, it was, it was, and surely homes deeper in the mountains were now burning.

She hoped everyone had enough straw.

GRETEL

Enough of this. She clapped her hands, changed out of her pajamas, and ate breakfast while watching the trailers come down the mountain. She sipped tea and sometimes said, *Just pretend it's foggy Ireland or Christmas* and *Please stop pretending and get up and do something real and useful. Change the story in your head.*

So she went outside and spray-painted a sign: FREE SHOWERS AND FOOD. PLACES TO PITCH A TENT. ALL WELCOME. She had a responsibility, after all: she was the first house at the base of the canyon and the simple fact of her location made her useful to others. As she lugged the plywood to the roadside to lean against a fence, she saw little Alexis in the distance. She was talking to a man standing outside his truck, which was pulling a boat. Then the two teenage horseback riders trotted up to them, and Alexis reached out her hand to touch the roan's nose, and then leaned in to press her face against the horse's chest in what could only be described as an act of deep adoration and yearning.

It made her smile but the stone was still in her throat because the thing was: the BB and her voice hadn't hurt the deer per se, but it had caused catastrophe. Who knows what had happened to that woman, or how much trouble the dent would cause, or how many toxins were now lodged in all their lungs, or if and how the mountainside would recover. Cause-effect. The ripple in the water. The consequences. And the foreknowledge of all that! She had predicted a thing. And that thing had happened.

And that's how all humans had lived all along. And it was just a fiery truth that everyone, everyone, everyone had known this was coming.

map sketched on a napkin

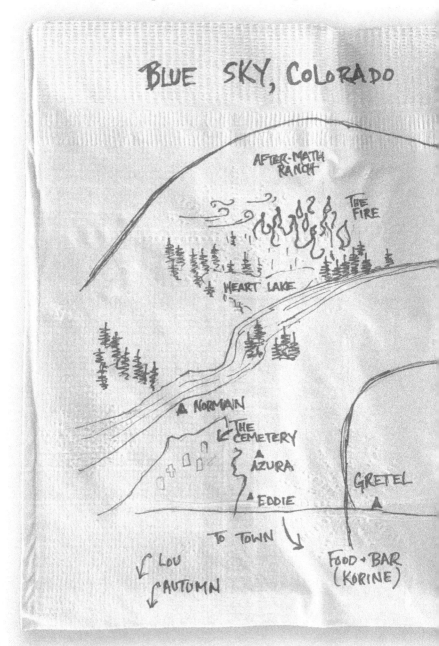

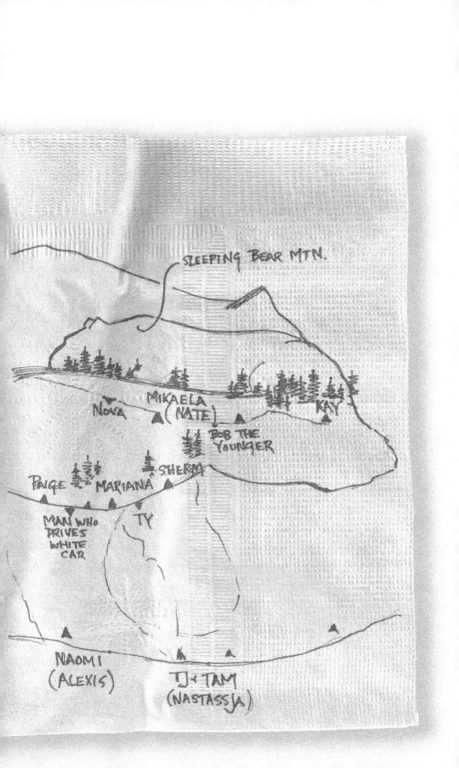

WOMAN

She'd have been looking out the kitchen window, watching smoke boil into sky. She'd have had the thought to leave… evacuation orders, helicopters, air as thick as milk. But the cats, the meadow, the thing her daughter called agoraphobia, so she would've shaken her head *no,* instead she'd go outside and move the sprinklers. The world was safe here, safe, safe, safe. So she would have looked at her hand on the doorknob and ducked her head. No, she wouldn't go. So she stood tall, sure of herself, at the threshold of the door, and that's where she must have sunk to her knees. Last inhale. Last exhale. Surely she closed her eyes and dreamed of rain and a greening world.

MOOSE

that creature standing there so forlorn-lorn-lorn these last years, but only because that creature has forgotten how to be, how to stand in meadow and tilt head to grass and wildflower and now she sinks and we both feel *cut, slice, fear* and i do not want to go dark, either, because all creatures = sharp desire to live.

    The desire to breathe.

    The desire to put hoof to earth   or wing to air.

          my great knees buckle   at the same time the creature falls too

             out of air   we both go down.

I have ancient feeling of standing in rain, nose in flowers.

RAVEN

besides air all i need is water which i find under the sprinkling water. Hunker, pant, rest, cat darts by, bear gimps by, one paw burned. moose goes down. woman goes down. trees go down. tree bits float up. woman ash floats up. moose ash floats up. I raise up. Wings, up, up, push, push, toward red poppies and brown cabin and blue bowl of water.

BEAR

and it was just a fiery truth that every creature, every one of them, all connected, all of them, all creatures could *sense* and thus had known this was coming. But only some could do something about it. The wild creatures were dependent on those tame creatures and those tame creatures failed. A den is now needed, a new den, new but it's all black smoldering and so she noses her aching paw burned on black and sleeps in a cottonwood crook by river dreaming of eating rosehips in a green meadow in spring.

Armadillo

HE'S BACK IN TEXAS NOW. YEAH, MAYBE HE HADN'T PUT OUT that fire at Heart Lake. He'd had a headache. From beer and altitude. He'd made a Good Faith effort—hadn't he? Used his camping pan filled with lake water, tossed it on the sizzle, sent ash flying into air. It's just this: he didn't want to go back for more and didn't want to use his drinking water since he'd need it for his hike out. And besides, it was a calm day, the campfire would cool off on its own accord. Because that's what fires should do. Though, sure, he coulda pissed on it at least. But— pause pause pause pause pause, open up that hard shell, look up at that Texas sky—maybe somewhere deep inside him, he supposes, he knew it was possible. That a fire would spring up. The thought *did* cross his mind as he hiked away, backpack pressing on his shoulders, headache pressing on his skull, a niggling feeling pressing on his heart—that vague uncomfortable sensation that surely all humans shared, which is, that, well, they could have done just a little bit better. But the moment passed, thank god. Armadillo means 'little armored one' after all, and so he did just that, knowingly, and went on with his day.

Grant_Application_From_ Hazardous_to_Moderate_ Gretel Kahne

Title of Grant Proposal: "From Hazardous to Moderate: Healing Land and Body after Megafires"

Alternate Title: "Funding Resistance Movements to Get You Fuckers Out." Another working title: "Grant Applications are built around a colonized, patriarchal system of education and if you really cared about getting grant money to diverse populations this whole process would be different, so please get that DEII statement off your website, you fuckers."

Significance and contribution:

I live on the evacuation perimeter of what is now Colorado's largest wildfire, which has been burning for months. The sheriff's deputy is outside my house, his lights turning red-blue-red, giving my house a strobe-light effect. As I write this, he is directing traffic as people race off the mountain with trailers filled with horses and goats and belongings. Although he can be a real ass, I'm glad for his existence for once.

I don't think you, the readers of this grant application (and I imagine you to be in D.C. or somewhere on the East coast), know how bad it is out here. I doubt any story I tell could convince you that you (meaning, those of you in D.C., in charge of grants) need to do something serious about climate change. My sister, who is an East Coaster, says she thinks of climate change about once a month. Let me tell you, we think of it every day. Because, every day, there are specific things we notice, because, after all, we are more influenced by space and terrain and the natural world, given that we have much more of it (50% of many Western states are public lands and about 8% of many Eastern states are public lands, so, you can see, we have a great gift that y'all don't, but also, that gift is being fucked up by bad policies, most of which come from you). There's a thing called The Proximity Principle. You don't see how we suffer because you're not nearby, so you aren't doing much, because you don't empathize. Which is why I'm writing this grant. I also hereby suggest the new center of government be relocated closer to the middle of this country—Colorado, maybe.

Anyway, people spray-painted their phone numbers on their animals and cut fences—the fire blew up again quickly this time—just hoping horses and cattle make their way to safety. On Facebook, people post things like "I found a roan horse and have it in my corral for its owner" or "able to board up to ten small animals." Most of my neighbors are fleeing for the *fourth* time since this fire began. It's exhausting. Our air quality is often listed as "Hazardous," though on some days, we are lucky to have "Moderate," a direction we could go in the largest sense, too—in terms of our forest management, our land health, and our wellness. (Or, we could go in the other direction, beyond "Hazardous" to "Dead Planet Stage" maybe).

So, my neighbors are really suffering. Nosebleeds and headaches. Helicopters and planes and sirens. Hacking coughs. Even the lung cancer diagnosis of a volunteer firefighter who was out in this junk a decade ago, so think of everyone ten years from now. We are breathing in more toxins than if we smoked a pack a day. I realize there is other suffering on the planet too, and I also think that sucks. This sucks. It all sucks. Can we please do something bigger and braver than all your bickering over little shit?

Some ass didn't put out a campfire up by Heart Lake. Imagine. It grew from one small campfire to one square foot, and from one square foot to one square mile. And now it is at 150,000 acres. Breaking record after record. Five new fires started in my area in one week. An incredible 1,016 wildfires burned in Colorado last year.

We know better than to expect any help from the government or otherwise. One should not expect help. We get it. We want to take care of ourselves. But also, we don't want to suffer the consequences of others' bad behaviors. And the bad behavior of this nation is causing us more than our fair share of suffering. So we're asking you fuckers to offer a helping hand and some semblance of justice. Environmental justice. Social justice. Like, maybe make your grant applications readable-and-doable by people who do not have your type of private school, colonizer education. Alert: There are other ways of knowing.

This is an exercise in mutual trickery, I'll admit it. I'm writing on behalf of my town for a grant to see if you'd be interested in giving us some money, so that we could turn around and give *you* some money, whether by bribing elected officials, or electing better officials, or funding a resistance movement, and so on, or so forth, whatever it takes to wean us off the fossil fuel industry. It could also be used for posting bond when we storm the offices of oil executives everywhere, but really, just kidding, I'm hoping to write a happy book about healing land and bodies, as I said I'd do. I'm hoping if these paragraphs look dense enough, you'll consider me qualified to receive a grant.

We are breathing in propane and chemicals and dead deer and we are very sick and very sad.

Grantor agency has assigned the following Agency Tracking Number to your application:
188865d827351382983988891383991931353820.

You will need to use this Agency Tracking Number when corresponding with the Grantor agency about your application. Use the Grants.gov Tracking Number at Grants.gov. We will provide 26 hours of educational webinars to clarify the login process. You can check your application's status and review your Agency Tracking Number.

Type: GRANT
    Grants.gov Tracking Number:
    GRANT13289dd849840929409420843209098432507072
    UEI: 000000000INDV0982098094325
    Application Name: Gretel Kahne
    Application Title: Healing Land and Body after Megafires
Message: The skies over D.C. look just fine. Really blue, in fact. Quit complaining. Alert: You chose to live near trees and all that nature stuff, after all.

Significance and contribution, continued

This is not just a story of my little community or my state—this is a story of much of our nation. California, Washington, Oregon, Montana, and Idaho are all suffering as well. I realize you have different issues out East, but I ask that you not only extend your empathy for those outside your purview, but that you fucking do something about it. Such as: ignore those oil and gas lobbyists! (And the NRA killers while you're at it!) Invest in alternate, green energies! Take this climate stuff seriously, you asses!

I know that numbers don't *mean* much to humans—we can't relate and they don't change our hearts—but I have heard I'm more likely to get a grant if I list some. And I do like science. So: the NIFC—the National Interagency Fire Center—reports that as of today, there have been 46,000 wildfires that have burned eight million acres *this year*, which is two million more acres than the ten-year average.

I apply for a Public Justice Fellowship to complete a book that puts a story to the suffering of evacuees and casualties and smoke jumpers and kids and firefighters, a story to the experience of scientists and health experts, and a story of where we might go from here. More specifically, I intend to present the scientifically-demonstrated ways in which nature heals the human body, and the ways in which humans can help heal this land. There is an inherent mutualism in healing.

Thank you for asking questions about how best to apply to the NEH Public Justice program, which we've just renamed the Insurmountable Program for Justice Seekers. Your application, From Hazardous to Moderate: Healing Land and Body after Megafires, has been assigned a new application number: FZ-27d0949829804—2640-0949941.

The NEH provides a website for applicants where you can check the status of your letters, send reminders to your letter writers, and view the program schedule. It is unlikely anyone will ever answer your questions. To log in, you must provide your NEH application number, FZ-279941 or FZ

390482457094 or FZ 23093480980, and also your Grants.gov tracking number, which is included in several email messages you received from Grants.gov. Also, your Grants.gov password is set to expire in 20 minutes.

It is this last point that will give the book its heartbeat—as we heal, we can help nature heal, and there is co-creation in this process. To that end, I would focus on specific instances of land/human recovery, such as the Wildland Restoration Volunteer group and the Youth Corp groups currently beginning restoration programs. History provides excellent examples of this as well—for example, in the 1930s, the CCC transformed the bodies of young men as they transformed the landscape with their labor. It was a reshaping of a body politic, literally. In part, this book will be a call to return to the wisdom of that approach. The physical labor of restoration will enhance our own restoration. As in, there are better and worse ways to heal from this, and better and worse long-term solutions, and I'd like to discuss that in my book.

I am called to write this book because, like the pandemic, these megafires present a *new type of suffering*—both for land and human. The suffering feels like experimentation. Requires new stories told in unique forms and techniques. We need to look to the past, understand our present, and mindfully approach our future—with fresh stories.

Thank you for your inquiry. Our office is currently closed due to COVID.

Final product and dissemination:

The tentative TOC looks like this:

Deer in the Poppies
Azimuth
One foot in the Black
Sleeping Bear Mountain
Obituary for a Wildfire
Solar Fire Interpretations Report
Crisis Hotline

And so on, and so forth. I'll likely involve some experimental form and technique—since creative approaches and imagination are what we need right now.

Sources:

Favorites include *The Nature Fix: Why Nature Makes Us Happier, Healthier, and More Creative* by Florence Williams; *Megafire: The Race to Extinguish a Deadly Epidemic of Flame* by Michael Kodas; *Braiding Sweetgrass: Indigenous Wisdom, Scientific Knowledge, and the Teaching of Plants* by Robin Wall Kimmerer; *Nature Love Medicine: Essays on Wildness and Wellness,* edited by Thomas Fleischner; *Forest Fires: Behavior and Ecological Effects* by Edward A. Johnson; *Fire Ecology of Pacific Northwest Forests* by James K Agee; *Between Two Fires* by Stephen Pyne. There is a host of general readership articles, such as: "The Healing Power of Nature" in *Time Magazine*; and various academic articles, such as "How does nature exposure make people healthier?: Evidence for the role of impulsivity and expanded space perception" in NIH's Library of Medicine (NIH/NLM). Also, some work by a little-known author named Laura Pritchett; she's super flawed and sometimes dense but good of heart; she does her best to capture the suffering she witnesses in her hometown and she does really love the West and the blue spinning ball we call home.

Conclusion:

As we hope for air quality to move from "hazardous" to "moderate" in the American West, we can simultaneously hope for that direction in the largest sense, too—in terms of our forest management, our land health, and our wellness. Or, better yet, new ways of living on this planet. May we discuss such non-discussable things as restraint, intergenerational equity, population numbers, economies built on ecological restoration, prospective survivors, and demolitions becoming renovations. And increase usage of the following words by 100%: climate crisis, climate chaos, climate change, climate realities, climate, planet, climate, planet, climate planet, respect for the nonhuman, and "one beautiful spinning ball we're wrecking." We had it all, didn't we? I hope you have a beautiful day on a beautiful planet! Thank you for reading this. Seriously.

Thank you for applying to the Public Justice competition and for your interest in the National Endowment for the Humanities and the U.S. Government. Unfortunately, your application *From Hazardous to Moderate: Healing Land and Body after Megafires AKA Funding Resistance to Get You Fuckers Out* (FZ-27994d3939q94001) has not been approved for funding.

We recognize that you invested considerable time in your application and want to assure you that your application received a careful and thorough review. We are typically only able to fund about .01% of the applications we receive to the program.

This year we received 26,987,638 applications and funded six, none of them having to do with the big elephant in the room, climate chaos. Don't be disappointed because, after all, people should not expect help, as you well know. Stand on your own two feet, even if you are bearing injustices, even if your suffering was caused by others, such as the oil execs who got our friends elected who got us these jobs. In power, we shall stay. We wish you the best with that fire of yours. Just don't breathe too deeply—that's our advice.

aspen trees serve
as an oracle to the sage

we breathe in, the opposite way of some,
we sense the heat first.
no, the furious wind first. then, hot heat.
Sense birds leave our branches. Beaks open, trying to cool.
Sense deer flow and leap by our trunks. Breathing.
Sense the bear pause, raise one paw. Breathing.
Sense our friends the pines, needles alight.
Feel tips of our own leaves curl.
Hear our sisters sing with stinging pain.
Rooted as we are, we gift our life energy downward into roots,
    into soil.
Come back, selves, we sing, *for in us, the root of true magic clings.*
Our livewire leaves shimmer as we blacken
and turn to ash.

After-Math Ranch

BOB SAT WITH HIS HEAD IN HIS HANDS BECAUSE THE FACTS wore him out: the wildfire had turned unexpectedly yet again and in the opposite direction predicted. This left the ranchers above him with barely enough time to cut fences, open gates, and *whoop* the cattle and horses out, trying to direct them into the roads and creek beds that would guide them down the mountain. Stock trailers were loaded with the best belongings, and as men and women and children abandoned their ranches and drove away, they sent sparks of wishes into the air: that unbranded calves would stay with their mamas, that instinct would lead the animals down to safety, that nature would show some pity and preserve all that they had worked for.

Those down-slope, the ones who had more time, put out a call for help. This call was repeated on the radio and was what Bob heard instead of the usual morning farm report. He sat at his kitchen table, fingertips rubbing his forehead hard, waiting for Ann to come out of the guest bedroom, which she might not do for a couple of hours, and listened to the plea for anyone with a stock trailer to meet at the school parking lot to help evacuate animals. As he stared into the crevices of his own palms, he decided that he would not go.

"What I'd like to see is a stream of stock trailers, one right after the other, climbing up that mountain pass," the radio announcer said. "Every time I hear the national anthem, my heart jumps up and salutes. That's how I'd feel to see such a sight. You know that feeling, I'm sure you do, so get out there and lend a helping hand. There's an estimated one thousand head up there, so it's gonna take nearly a hundred trips to get those animals out."

Bob figured Eddie was on his way already. They'd spoken of the fire this morning over at the donut shop, shrugging off the most recent tally of how many structures were lost and wincing at the report that a cluster of cattle had been engulfed in flames.

"I know whatcha mean," the waitress had said to their response. "A cow worth a couple a hundred bucks is harder to take than all them million dollar houses being burnt up, isn't it?"

You bet it is, they agreed. The livestock and wild animals—well, that was a shame. So was the plight of the ranchers and farmers losing outbuildings and homes and corrals—Jesus, all that work—as if living a life of calloused hands wasn't hard enough. Also, they felt sorry for the hippies, the ones that lived up the canyon in small A-frames and double-wides to escape the rest of humankind, which was something Bob and Eddie could surely sympathize with. What they didn't find hard to take was the loss of the glass-and-wood cabins cluttering up the mountainside for the rich folks' weekends away from Denver. Bob was relieved to see those houses burnt to a crisp. Serves 'em right, he said, to which Eddie agreed, adding that those folks probably needed some trauma and heartbreak in what he imagined were their otherwise soft-hand lives. That's what Eddie called folk like that, Soft-Hands.

They weren't naïve enough to discount the fact that they felt sorrier for the people most like themselves—humans are apt to do that, is what Bob said to Eddie, who nodded and said, "Ain't that the truth." But no matter what they thought, he added, nature had more rights than people and their too-fancy homes—more rights than anybody, in fact—and it was good of her to give a reminder once in awhile, to put humans in their place.

§

Well, he wouldn't go. Heck with it all, he thought, which was the same thing he'd been thinking a lot recently. He didn't feel good, for one thing, and only in the last few months had it become clear that it's nearly impossible to care about anything when the body aches. He knows that his aches are minor on the scale of human suffering, and yet they're enough to make him feel drained. His stomach's been bothering him, and not the little sort of tummy ache the idiot doctor thinks he's talking about, but the serious unbearable pain of a heavy weight lodged beneath his ribs. He's supposed to eat bland foods and sip at tea and forgo the alcohol. These are not changes he's prepared to make, but he also hopes to claw himself out of this stupor.

He finally took his hands away from his head and pulled the morning paper and a pen toward him. In the margin, he meant to make a list of the things he should do. Instead, he stared at the fringe of the thin paper until he heard Ann, who then shuffled into the kitchen and slumped into a chair beside him. She was wearing a white robe and she ran her pale fingers through her carefully cut dark hair.

The fact that she got up so late every morning was the cause of a sheepishness she projected until he said what she wanted him to, which was, "What the hell, it's your vacation." So he said it, and she perked up, her head lifted with the poise and aloofness he was used to.

She'd told him she'd flown out to Colorado to see her big brother, but it was clear the visit had more to do with escaping something in Boston. A tiny part of him hoped that was the case; he admitted he was glad to see her suffer a bit. But no, maybe such a wish was just the result of his hurt feelings. She'd never had much interest in the brother who stayed home and ranched instead of going to an East-coast college, who hadn't married rich (Ann's husband was the king of the Soft-Hands, is what Bob told Eddie), the misfit brother who didn't care much about fashion or the conveniences of life.

She'd only written a handful of times in all the years she'd been gone, never acknowledged the birthday cards he sent her, and only made a brief appearance at his daughter's and wife's funerals. Only once, soon after she'd moved back east, had she called and invited him to come visit. He'd done this, even though he knew what she wanted, which was the chance to show off her beautiful, clean, fancy home. To show him she'd come quite a way, to which he could only agree. She wanted something more from him then, some recognition that she was the better person for the life she had made. This he refused to give. In his comments and compliments, he refused to say that she and her life were superior to his, that days spent in an office were better than those on a tractor, that a new leather couch was better than a dog hair-covered old one. He refused to say this because although she hoped this was true, he knew it was not. She was here because she wanted something again, though he wasn't sure what. He suspected something had worn thin in her life, that the heat that prodded her on was dissipating. And he couldn't help suspecting that she'd come to comfort herself with his discomfort, to measure the distance between them again.

He wasn't all that interested in obliging her this time either. But he slid a coffee cup over to her and filled it. She mumbled a thank you, and they sat quiet for awhile, until Ann said, "Oh," and tilted her head toward the radio. He hadn't been listening any longer, but he realized she had been, and her face had taken on a look of concern. He scowled and looked away. He was disgusted with her, with the radio announcer, with the whole human race for this fake concern. She felt nothing for these ranchers and animals, and why should she? It was a rare case when people cared about things they were unconnected to.

He saw he was right. He watched her face flit between concern and self-centered sleepiness, and never once did she lift her eyes to him with an inquiring look, wondering if they should answer the call for help. What she finally said was, "Will the fire get here?"

"No."

"Are you sure?"

"Yes. No. Yes. Depends. I don't know. I guess I should go up there, but I'm not feeling so good today."

"Did you take your medicine?"

"No."

"Why not?"

"It doesn't work."

"It *should* work. That's what it's for. I think you should see another doctor. That's what I'll do today. I'll make you another appointment. Is that all right with you?"

He didn't say anything, but he felt himself rock a bit with assent, and felt her surprise.

"Okay, then." She shuffled off in her slippers to his desk in the living room, and he was left to listen to the reports of the fire, of wind shifts, of the crew's weariness. Goddamn, he should go up and help, he knew it. Well, if he could muster the energy to go, he'd tell whoever was in charge—probably Autumn, that busybody with all the weird new signs she kept putting up in her yard—that he was willing to haul cattle and workhorses.

It was because of Ann that he hated the rich out of proportion to what made sense, he knew, perhaps because he equated her wealth with her neglect. That's what he wanted, of course. Some acknowledgment of *his* life. Something about how gorgeous the landscape was, how hard he worked, how relaxed and easy he was on a horse. How *he*, at least in some respects, was the one with the life worth coveting.

If she did say such a thing, he'd go ahead and admit that she'd been brave to leave the ranch, to learn about and build a new life. But they were too different now to try to appreciate and understand the other in the sort of way that takes effort and time—no, he doubted if either of them had enough strength and energy for that now.

§

When the call came, he wasn't surprised much. As he listened to Eddie yelling over the buzz of his cell phone and the bawling of cattle, Bob looked at his sister, sitting on the couch, hunched over her cell phone. He glanced toward the kitchen window that faced the mountains, which was the direction Eddie was calling from. A billowing cloud of dark smoke rose like a mushroom cloud above a far slope of trees and spread like a fan in the air.

"I'm at the After-Math Ranch," Eddie was saying. "The Austens' place."

"Yeah, yeah, I was on my way up anyway. Just now. I'll drive straight up." That's what he said, but he wanted to say that he'd just had it with this world, and didn't anyone else get like that, just fed up and tired? Didn't they ever get to a point where they couldn't even be shamed into caring, because there was just nothing nothing nothing inside?

He left Ann curled up and hugging herself, and went outside and backed up his pickup to the red stock trailer. He rubbed his stomach and poured a handful of Tums into his mouth, a bottle of which rattled around with all the other junk on the seat. Just as he was pulling away, Ann came running out, waving for him to stop. She was dressed, now, wearing jeans and a white t-shirt and ballcap.

"I want to come," she said. "If I'd known you were going, I would have asked to come along."

He regarded her for a minute. "Out of guilt or curiosity?"

"Oh, Bob, I know what you're thinking. I came home to see *you*. Maybe out of guilt, maybe out of curiosity, who the hell knows." She walked to the passenger side and opened the door. "So can I come or what?"

He reached out his hand to help pull her into the truck, and then, so that the anger might be smoothed over, he began to talk. "We're going to the After-Math Ranch. A retired math professor owns it. Get it? But it has another meaning, too, because 'after-math' is the stubble after a crop's been cut."

"Clever. It might have a third meaning after this fire." She laughed, and because, perhaps, she feared her comment was not appropriate, she grew solemn. "I hope not, though."

"Oh hell." He was surprised by the edge in his voice and was relieved when Ann laughed again.

"I should care, shouldn't I?" She rubbed her temples and closed her eyes. "I'm having a hard time caring about anything these days. Something's wrong with my humanity."

Here's where they were still a bit alike, that's what he wanted to say then, but before he could form the words, she was talking again. "Though every once in a while people surprise me," she said. "Look at this."

Ahead of them was a line of trailers that wound up the canyon as far as they could see, a couple miles at least, he figured, of pickups and trailers back-to-back. The sight *did* make his throat feel tight with pride, mostly because he could show off this bit of community generosity to his sister.

"We got horse people," he said, lifting his finger off the steering wheel and pointing to a fancy new trailer in front of them, which was being pulled by a matching truck, both painted with swirls of turquoise. "And we got cattle people." Now he pointed at the trailer in front of it, a beat-up brown thing that looked much like his own.

"Money," she said.

"Yep," he said. "We still don't talk wealth much in this country, though we sure as hell get hung up on other things. I don't believe a rich person and poor person can be true friends."

"And if someone thinks they can, I bet you it's the richer

person who thinks so." She laughed. "Oh, Bob, even I can see that, even from where I'm at."

He felt a sudden surge of gratitude. Her words weren't much, really, but after these years of almost nothing, they seemed like enough.

§

They didn't speak much the rest of the drive, except to comment on a speeding white car that nearly killed them, and it was the radio announcer who kept the silence from being difficult. The information his animated voice conveyed was interesting to them both, simply because it was new, and perhaps because it involved pain for someone else. Before evacuating houses, the announcer said, homeowners should put a sprinkler on the roof, cut away trees and brush, dig a ditch, pull up all the plants. "It's called a defensible space, folks," said the announcer. "Create this space if you have the time."

"Defensible space," Ann said. "That's a fine idea."

He could have told her that he understood, but instead he looked out the window at the river curling alongside the road. Usually there were rafters and kayakers, folks fly fishing and families having picnics, but now the river was deserted and there was only the low water, tumbling down rocks and pooling near the banks. But it was the sky that caught his attention when they rounded a corner. Ahead was the billowing dark smudge against the backdrop of a bright blue sky.

"Oh, god!" Ann breathed. "All that from our Heart Lake Fire. Oh, god. That's horrible."

"I used to camp there a lot." He remembers the feel of pulling up a trout, knowing he'd have it for dinner around a campfire, how the mountain sheep gazed at him as he ate, how the remnants of burned tinfoil and singed lemon slice was one of the best things in his entire life. This is one of the many stories he would have liked to have told her soon after it happened. He had practiced telling her the story in his mind, and when he told Eddie and others about it, he imagined he was telling Ann instead. It was silly of him to want to impress her with his life, like he had way back when he'd put the worm on her hook or had her big-eyed at the story of a mountain lion he'd seen— those times when they'd clung together because they were two lonely ranch kids with cranky parents and a lot of work to do and not much to make them feel special. Crazy, a grown man still wanting acknowledgment, interest, love from his sister. But she didn't seem interested in his story, so he concentrated on the road ahead and let the silence seep between them.

The radio announcer was describing the county fairgrounds, filled with rescued livestock. Ranchers from all over the state were offering free pasture for animals, free hay, opening their homes to displaced folks. "It's not the fire that's such a sight to see," the announcer said. "It's the people swarming to help, that's the thing worth noticing here."

§

When Bob pulled into the After-Math Ranch, an old trailer was already backed up to the corral and Eddie and another man were pushing the back door closed on a load of cattle. Bob let his truck idle until the other driver, who he didn't recognize, drove away. Each man lifted his fingers off the steering wheel in a muted wave as they passed one another. Then Bob backed up his own trailer, following Eddie's gestures.

Bob climbed out of the truck and was surprised by the strength of the smell. The air didn't look particularly smoky, although bits of ash floated past his eyes, but the smell of scorched earth was strong. The cows in the corral were bawling, and there was a distant buzz of airplanes, one of which was sending an orange plume of stuff down as it banked to the right. The hot sunlight and the noise made him feel dizzy. He leaned against the pickup for a moment, bowing his head to regain his balance.

"Glad you came."

"I was on my way."

"Some Search and Rescue guy took my truck down a while ago. I told him I'd stay and load the rest of the cows for as long as I could. He didn't look so good, Bob."

Eddie's face was full of sweat and there were so many rivulets of moisture that Bob was struck with a sudden worry for him. He reached into his truck for a jug of water and handed it to Eddie, who tilted it up above him, letting the water flow into his mouth and across his face. "You don't look so good yourself," Bob said.

"The Search and Rescue guy looked like he was about to keel over. He's been working round the clock."

"Hard for him, I reckon."

"And Mr. Austen being in the care facility and all. My Lord. I made the whole family go, his kids and nieces and such, take my truck down. Do you think I did right?"

"Sure," Bob said, but only because he had no other words to offer, and because he wasn't sure whether it was better to stand strong and fight a futile battle or get the hell out. If he knew that, he'd know what to do with his own life.

"Guess we better get a move on," Eddie said. "This'll be the last load. They told us to get out twenty minutes ago. Fire's close for sure, but I don't think we're in any real danger."

"Naw." Bob turned to follow Eddie toward the pens, but then stopped and turned toward Ann, to see, perhaps, if he had her consent to stay, or if she was frightened, or to see if she had been listening at all.

She was still sitting in the truck, looking toward the house and the plume of black smoke above it, her mouth open in an O and a stunned and sorrowful look on her face.

§

As Bob and Eddie rounded up the cattle, Bob heard the slam of the truck's door. Ann was walking toward the house, cocking her head and looking uncertain. She emerged a moment later carrying a small coffee table, then later with a painting and a quilt, all of which she loaded into the bed of the truck. Soon she was walking quickly between house and truck, running almost, and for a moment she did not look like a well cared-for woman, someone who lived in a house that cost as much as his entire ranch, but someone who was afraid, who was working hard out of necessity and fear, laboring for survival. As he *he-yaawd* at the cattle and flapped his arms at the cows who tried to back out of the trailer, he watched her jog, faster and faster, from house to truck. On one trip, she emerged from the house with something that looked like an old sewing machine table, which looked similar to one their mother had owned. Ann was bowed backwards with the weight of it and still walked as fast as she could, jerking and stumbling, and he wanted to rush and help her. He couldn't, though; he was leaning against a cow's rear to encourage her to step up into the trailer, and if he let up on the pressure, the cattle would turn and bolt out of the trailer. He could only watch and wince as Ann strained under the weight, frightened by the way she lurched toward the truck.

Just as Bob was pushing the trailer door shut, a calf darted, slipping away between two fence poles. As he and Eddie dodged around the corral trying to get her in, Bob remembered his grandfather telling him about the war, how the worst part was the screaming of a colt that had its back legs blown off. They had agreed that humans could inflict whatever evils they desired on each other, but that animals ought to be left out of it. Some animals screamed, and some suffered silently and dumbly, which was how he imagined the death of two cows who'd gotten stuck in a ditch bank and frozen last winter. Humans did that, screamed or suffered silently, maybe depending on the situation or the individual soul. Oh Jesus, how he'd like to tell Ann that he was sorry she had pain going on inside her. He'd say, I got some of my own troubles, too. We seem to be the quiet sort, or quiet is what our particular distress calls for, who knows? But we're hurting, nonetheless.

He felt sick, still. The smell of diesel from his truck mixed with the smoke, and his stomach felt empty and he wished he had taken in a bit less coffee this morning. He should have slept in a little later, like his sister, instead of rising with the sun. Most of all, he wished he could sit down, for just a minute, in some cool, quiet place with clean air. He forced the last calf in, pressing her against the others already in the trailer. The cows bawled and kicked, and the ones on the edges put their noses out of the slats and snorted as the men pushed the back door closed behind them.

"It's for your own damn good," Eddie grunted as he locked the back of the trailer. "We're trying to save your ugly asses."

Bob chuckled. "You gonna ride back with us, or face the fire?"

"I'll take a ride with you, if you'll have me," Eddie said. "I already opened the gates for whatever cows are left. Let's get the hell out of here."

They both stood for a moment, catching their wind and wiping sweat from their faces. Bob was hot clear through, and he couldn't tell if the heat came from him or if the fire was getting closer. In any case, he wanted to get away, get down to his own ranch and sit by the coolness of the river. As he walked to the front of the truck, he could see that Ann had loaded up quite a bit. Lamps and boxes full of knickknacks were coated in a thin layer of ash. As he climbed in the truck beside her, he saw that the hair on her brow was wet, and she too was sucking in air in an effort to catch her breath. She was staring at a lamp in her lap, one that looked like it was made of stained glass.

"Nice of you," he said, nodding at the lamp.

She nodded but didn't speak. He thought she looked on the verge of tears, and so he busied himself with starting the truck. She had to move closer to him to make room for Eddie, who squeezed in on the other side. "Watch out for these," she said as she moved closer. She nodded at a jumble of animal figurines dressed up in fancy clothes. They were crammed into the seat between them and Bob considered, for a brief instant, what sort of strange world produced porcelain rabbits in hoop skirts and how they came to be staring up at him from a seat littered with bits of hay and pieces of cows' ear tags and bailing twine.

As he drove away from the After-Math Ranch and turned onto the main road, he saw the billowing smoke of fire in his rearview mirror and where smoke met land, an orange glow bloomed into the air. He knew then that the ranch would indeed burn, and tears started of their own accord, and he didn't swipe them away. None of that gruffness was real. He felt for every damn person, and it was the hurt that was making him mean because he just couldn't take it. But he had to concentrate: the truck was heavy with cattle, and he had to shift to a lower gear and concentrate on the curves. They passed a sheriff's deputy heading up the canyon with its sirens going, then caught up with the line of trailers snaking down the mountain with horses' tails or cows' sides showing through the back doors and side windows.

Ann held the lamp with one hand and rubbed at her eyes with the other, and Eddie kept wiping the moisture from his forehead. After a while, though, he felt their breathing even and their bodies cool, and now they were listening not to their pounding hearts, but to the sound of porcelain animals clinking against one another and the cattle bawling from the trailer.

"Tonight there'll be quite a sunset," Bob said quietly. "Sad to think of it that way, isn't it? But that smoke will make the sunset so red, streaks of orange and red above those blue mountains."

"I didn't think of that." Ann breathed out, then, and with that breath there seemed to be some sort of surrender, some release of a tightness within her. She said, "Maybe devastation is the beginning of something? We gotta do this whole thing better, maybe?"

Bob nodded. He looked in his rearview mirror at the fire chasing livestock and wild game and humans down the canyon. Things that should never come close were being funneled together, and he wondered whether such an event could save them.

Abelardo

YOU HAPPENED TO BE BORN IN EL PETÉN. JUNGLE-rainy-wet-Guatemala. Now on your way to Rock Springs. Hot-dry-wind-Wyoming. Twenty-four dollars an hour on construction. Plus a bonus for staying in Salt Lake City since housing. There being hardly any. You didn't use a coyote because here's the truth of life: better to go alone. No moral stress of sharing your water, or not. So you, Lalo, cross at Piedras Negras in Coahuila and swim the river and jump the train to San Antonio and think of your two hijos sleeping on woven mats, dirt floor, cinder block home, sounds of parrots and monkeys outside.

2,693 miles solo.

Not quite there, todavía no, ya merito.

Made it to Denver, then Fort Collins, some old Fort, taking land from others, fort fort military fort. Now you're supposed to be on the way to Laramie, bus, onward. But the friend-of-a-friend, the one who was to drive you, well, a wildfire is coming. And she was alone, too alone, in her efforts to flee her cabin with the sound of a braying donkey and bleating goats outside. So now you are helping her, encouraging a donkey into a trailer. Time is running short. The fire is coming. You keep your eye on the sheriff's lights, blue-redding the sky down the street. You would prefer to be by yourself. But when you close your eyes while drinking from the gallon of water, you see moving dots of people, gente de todo el mundo, swarms of dots, everyone moving to safety, to some version of green pasture, to what they hope is seguridad.

one foot in the black

which is generally good advice and also the motto of us smoke-jumpers. Keep one foot in the black.

Which means: head toward a burned area, should you need to escape. Means, our nervous systems are wired to turn and run, and you need to be cognizant of an escape route, which is why Leticia says I'll never make a good romantic partner. Always ready to turn and run.

I say to her: whatcha talking about, you joking me? You know as well as I do what it's like to *step into sky*. Talk about trust and commitment. And the necessary crazy! We are smoke-jumpers!

She laughs and says: true that, Veltry.

We gather our gear. Head out onto the tarmac. It's hot as hell, but the wind is calm at the moment.

There were those twelve-or-so smokejumpers that died in Colorado in '94. They died by fire, burned under their foil blankets, but in reality, they died by wind. No, not just wind. Jumping, gusting, *living* wind, and plenty of oral stories from those who have come from cultures closely tied to the land, such as my friend Norman, whose grandfather was Northern Ute, and who will tell you that wind is conscious, it's alive, it's a force to be reckoned with, and that is what made me think of oral stories anyway, of me just recording stories rather than writing them because some of us aren't writers but we have stories to tell, which is why I'm recording this. Anyway, those people had fire retardant dropped right *on them* and still, they burned. I cannot describe the heart stab I feel when I think of it. It burns hotter than a fire in my heart.

We duck ourselves onto the plane. Leticia has developed a sad and resigned wind on the inside. Sure, it's because of COVID and wildfires and warring men. She's really had it with testosterone, as she puts it. But I think also it's because of me. A relationship five years in and it's at the point she'd love to see some spunk and energy and commitment, and she doesn't see that radiating off me, so I'm quietly breaking her heart. That's a different kind of ache than the ache for the world at large. The heart is capable of all sorts of variations of achy burns. She thinks I have one foot in the black.

While I like calm people, this new way of hers is just *too* calm. Like a moment in a day when all the birds quit chirping and everything's too still and you look up, pretty sure something bad is about to happen.

The plane takes off, a little rocky, but fine enough. We sit side by side, knees touching. It was in 1939 that the USFS first used smokejumpers. My grandfather was one, in fact. A conscientious objector. And half Black, too. So, unusual, especially for that time. After the war, there were all these extra parachutes and so on, and it was a good way to fight fires, especially those in the most remote regions. In the 1930s through the 1960s, there was this idea of total suppression. Fire, out. That was the motto. The mass production of fire lookouts started after the Great Fire of 1910, in which 87 people were killed. That's when the fire detection really started, and 30 years later, people were stepping out of planes to help put them out.

The history of firefighting is worthy of a book unto itself. You'd see now we are at a turning point. Because this early idea of *all fires out* was wrong. It had a lot of good ideas in it, but a lot of wrong ones, too. Things have changed as we figured it out.

More nuanced approach. More rules. More protocol. Not loved by all. Used to be, to be a smokejumper, your main job requirement was just to love the outdoors. Plus be fit, strong, and crazy. A bit of a daredevil.

These days, it's way less wild-west. Lot of forms. Lot of training. Lot of meetings. Probably a lot more thinking.

But still, there's this one wild component: Do you know what it's like to drop 1,500 feet from an airplane? And five seconds later, your parachute explodes alive? So orchestrated. And yet, so fucking not. Orchestrated and yet wild. Like love.

That's what I lean over and tell Leticia. Who gives me her kind, slightly crooked-teeth smile, though it is also a tense smile because she is about to jump, and jumping comes with fear, even if you've done it plenty before. Bona fide and roaring fear.

Her resigned sadness worries me. I would know better how to react if it was anger. Or bitterness. Or departure. But sad? That affects me like nothing else. Which is why I went to my friend Norman a few months ago. Norman Who Makes Things, that's what I call him. I asked him for a little help in getting Leticia's sadness out.

My father was there, digging trenches, all those years ago, when those men died. My father happened to be a little farther away. Fire doesn't travel downhill as fast as uphill, so he made the crest and ran like a madman down. He just outran it. He was lucky that way. Norman Maclean wrote that famous book, *Young Men and Fire*, about another disaster up in Montana. Thirteen men. One of his main points was that wildland firefighters simply shouldn't be put into mountains with steep slopes at certain times. Say, like, when a cold front is coming, which is going to make winds high and unpredictable. Canyon winds are no joke; they are alive. If you wanna have your heart broke, listen to "Cold Missouri Waters" by James Keelaghan 'bout the one of two who survived, how he struck a match to waist-high grass and stepped inside it, lay face down, stayed inside the black, you see. But then, it happened again, like with my father in Colorado: four women and ten or more men, each paying the price of wind.

Which is why they are being so careful with us. Still, this fire is doing a number on my nervous system. It's going on and on and *on*. When people say, the biggest wildfire in Colorado, they are just trying to put some frame around the situation, which is pretty unframeable. It's just fucking huge, a wild monster.

Fire itself is normal and good, but this? This fire is not normal or good.

I remember once, before Leticia got sad, when she was still fighting for us to be an amazing couple, or whatever it is people fight for in that regard, she said, Relationship is work! To which I replied, I know, hon, we are the laborers, not the recreators. Meaning, people like us, we get to know the backcountry, the most remote and beautiful places, in the True way. Not in the way a backpacker gets to know it. No, we have a *result* in mind, we are doing something that will aid the planet. That's why laborers don't like the recreators, of course—that tension will go on forever. To our mind, it has to do with giving back, *doing* something. Of use. For the greater good. I suppose I see their point of view, too, though. And there's no reason to pit ourselves against one another. We humans should quit doing that.

But Leticia knew what I meant: easy dating is like a backpacker. Recreator. Long love is like a smokejumper. Laborer.

We look at each other now. Hold hands. I run my thumb along the side of hers. As you might imagine, her hand is rough from rough work. We're getting close now. We bump around through the sky. What a view. Watersheds and scree. The sheer rock granite walls of the canyon and the famous Ingleside Formations just one canyon north and how, generally speaking, the Rocky Mountains of Colorado stretch into Wyoming where they'll taper into more wrinkly mounds.

If only the camper had called the fire in before it blew up, I say.

If only the camper had put the fire out in the first place, she says.

Love you, Leticia, I say.

Here we go, she says.

Adrenaline, I say.

Dopamine, she says.

The plane hits a pocket of air and we pitch to the side, then the pilot banks the plane because there's the meadow. Another bump.

One of the first female lookouts was Ethel Caldwell in 1920, and her octagon was dismantled and replaced by a pre-cut cabin designed in 1929 by the Northern Rocky Mountain Experiment Stations. Carried in by mules. I mention this because you can see how long Americans have been trying to put out fires, which is partly the reason we are having such trouble now. That, and climate change. Bark beetles. Dead forests. High winds. Low precipitation. But I also want to point out that women have been part of it more than most people imagine. Leticia is a badass. Which is one of the many reasons I love her.

Fire has kept humans warm. Fire has regenerated landscapes. Fire has helped meadows grow. Love does all this too. Keeps us warm, growing, regenerating. I say to all: let fire burn, let love burn.

So, yeah, in conclusion, let me say: We're gonna have to change, i.e., let fires burn; indeed, we're going to have to do prescribed burns. People don't like it, but people can be real dumdums, which is the most polite way I know how to say it. We need a whole shift about the way we think about not overeacting to fire, so that there can be healthy fires, so that we don't have huge monsters. It's progress. Although it's also just going back in time, because during the course of human history, mostly, we let nature run her course. Although I realize it's not that simple, since nature wouldn't have lit many of these fires anyway. Most fires, including this one, being caused by humans.

The spotter tosses paper streamers out the door and they fall to the meadow and there's the shouting of the final check, a slap on the back. I fix my eyes on the horizon. Sit in the open door.

Jump.

The wind yanks my body like a raven blown backward.

My belly sinks as the skin on my cheek ripples up.

Look. The world is silent.

I pull the release, the parachute deploys.

Whoosh.

And now I can hear. And now, weightless, I am shaking. The meadow is nearing.

Float. Hands on steering guides, I tug on the left as the jump spot nears.

Breath catches. Noise escapes my throat, bite on mouthguard. The fire to the east with its big billowy plume. I'm meandering down through the sky, floating down to the crazy-beautiful tops of trees, who are looking up at me, saying, *Save us. Do something.*

Movement catches my eye. A moose trotting through forest. But I gotta turn so as to face the wind.

Then, oof. Toes touch. Swing my hips around, feet together, feet on ground. Roll to my side. Roll to my back. Rise. Strip the jumpsuit, roll up chute, shoulder gear; meanwhile, above, the plane circles back toward this meadow. Here she comes.

I move fast as I can, just as I rehearsed in my mind, so that when Leticia lands, there I am, unfettered, ready, on bended knee, with the ring Norman made.

She stands there, panting, catching her breath.

I gulp air. Hot and smoky air. It's a strange noise, fire at a distant roar, and I take a breath to hear it. I straighten my pack.

Our eyes meet, hold steady.

She doesn't answer. We have but just a second. But then, a laugh-gasp belts from her mouth. She looks over at the bloom of smoke and looks back into my eyes.

She says, What about one foot in the black?

Dang lady, I say, still on bended knee. Dang, we also keep one foot in the green. The living part.

You sure you mean this, Veltry? she says.

I do, I say.

Then I do, she says.

I stand and hold her tight and fast because we gotta move. We gotta change how we do things. We gotta look ahead. Do the right thing. So the future plays out like we want. Middle of wilderness, parachute at feet, plane above, we both stand with boots on earth.

Azimuth

Azimuth:

noun

the direction of a celestial object from the observer, expressed as the angular distance from the north or south point of the horizon to the point at which a vertical circle passing through the object intersects the horizon. The horizontal angle or direction of a compass bearing.

You say: I have the smoke report when you're ready.

You wait for them to say: go ahead.

You peer through the Osborne's bull's eye from the lookout and concentrate. You report the township, section, azimuth of the smoke. Without the azimuth, it makes no sense—everything is too vague and therefore unhelpful.

What I've learned about life: specificity of location, of words, of intention. Without it, you float around, your whole life through, being unhelpful to everyone, including yourself.

You offer a description of the smoke: the size, color, drift direction, fuel type. You wonder about all our souls, intersecting with each another. You wonder about deer running past blackening aspen, trying to not intersect with white trunks. You wonder about the trees sending nutrients into the soil; they know death is coming. You wonder about microbes in the soil—more life in a teaspoon of that than there are humans on earth. You wonder about the crisscross of roots and fungi and nematodes. Then you look up. At the celestial objects. The fact that there is a specific *you* at this specific *moment* in the universe taking one single *breath* blows you away. Despite all the sorrows and troubles, it is a fucking miracle. You, the azimuth for the stars, and they for you.

True line of latitude

NATE LOOKS THROUGH THE WINDOW AT THE NIGHT SKY—
the last time, he realizes, he'll see it from this vantage point,
from Nastassja's window. He seeks out a planet or a big star—
Polaris, perhaps. He needs some bright firm thing to hold what
he is feeling because she will not hold it—she is not even aware
of it—and even if she was, she would reject the notion of
steadying him through it, and even though she says steady steady
steady to the horses, she does not offer it to him.

Please, he says. It's moot. I don't wanna talk about this anymore.

Not good enough, she whispers, for fear of waking her parents up. She smells of the horses and of wildfire smoke and
whiskey. Tell me your version of why we're ending.

He keeps his head tilted away from her, on the stars, hoping
it will settle the spinning room. Smoke's cleared, he says. Check
out them stars. Maybe tonight will be the night that the fire gets
contained. Or maybe it will miraculously just…go out. End. The
End.

That last bit gives him pause—oh, the irony. How we want
some things to just end, but not others.

Just tell me, Nate.

He sighs. Shhh. Your parents will hear us. Okay. We just
ended, okay? Fine. Let's say it's because you feel numb. Let's call
it good with that. Neither of us will say anything negative to our
friends at school. It's all cool.

That's why we're ending? Because I feel numb?

That's what you said. You're just drunk. I know that's only one version of the story. There are many stories. Many reasons.

She makes a whimper and curls up next to him. Please, sweethoney.

Nastassja, he says, drawing out the name he's found beautiful since he met her near the lockers at the high school. It's my memory. Let it rest. I'm tired, and you're even more tired. And we're both drunk.

Tell me anyway, she says. I can't quite remember.

Why bother? It's over, done. It doesn't matter.

No, tell me.

I dunno! Wildfire! COVID! Climate change! It all presses down and things just...dissipate. But when she begs, he says, Because today we saw the footage from the command center, and your family's cabin is gone. The winds were terrible today, weren't they? First one way, then the other, gusts in every direction. Why was the wind so angry, do you think?

My grandfather's cabin.

Yes. It burned. We saw it there, burned. We should name the winds. In other countries, they name winds. And winds have personalities, god-like powers. And if the Earth is to be saved—and it won't be, it's too late, but if it were to be saved—it will be through the imagination. It would be because we made up stories about wind. You know?

Adults think we don't care about the past, about history, but that's not true. Then she adds, That's where we first had sex.

Made love, he corrects.

She grunts, affirmative. Then adds, Wow, the cabin is just gone, really gone, burned, and somebody left that campfire unattended up at Heart Lake. I'd shoot him if I could. If I knew who it was, I'd shoot him. I'm so angry at stupid adults in a stupid world run by stupid businesses. Bet it was a rich ass from Texas.

Yeah, he says. I hear you.

I don't personally want to shoot anyone, I guess. Not really. But one thing I'd do, truly do, is help conscientious killers hide and feed them and stuff. Like, be a support system for Earth Saviors. I wanna write a play about that.

She shifts her head onto a new spot on his shoulder and he gets caught up in fingering strands of her hair and wonders if he should sneak down the hallway and get her some saltine crackers from the kitchen, if she'll be sick, but he is unwilling to move, and he's got to keep his eye on those stars.

She says, Plus the fire will be over someday, and then I won't be numb again anymore.

Her voice sounds so hopeful. What can he do with that except look up at the stars? He is drunk still so he's able to say, I wish so much you loved me. Just to be certain, just to say it aloud, you're clear on this? You're not in love? You're still not in love? It's just not love?

Naw, she mumbles from his lap. I just can't make myself feel somethin'.

So the reason we're ending is, You feel nothing. You're numb.

She's asleep now, though, with her head now nestled on his shoulder. He considers how his DNA is more…delicate…which is why, yeah, he'd like to shoot the fucker who started the fire for ruining everything. He could do it. The anger is that high. The sky darkens and he flips his fingers through her hair and smears some tears and tells himself to get his feet under him because, by god, he has some traveling to do when school is done and he has nothing to tether him to this godforsaken burning town, he is going to find someone who wants to love, and be loved, and who is tender and alive and kind. He's got to get away from this fire. This wind. This fucked up world. He's got to get away from the anger directed at the fire, and, really, at her.

It doesn't matter the reasons she doesn't love him, because

it leads to the same conclusion, which is that she doesn't love him.

The true line of latitude, he heard, involves the sighting of Polaris, which allows surveyors to complete their latitude and head due west. Every thirty-six miles you close corners and start again.

He decides to close corners and start again. It's in the thirty-six that one can get lost, go slightly astray. There's nothing to be done. She doesn't love him—she's a few degrees off heart-center, is all, and the wind will never blow her back. And that is that. That is how the stars line up.

Dirt:
A Terra Nova Expedition

Part of a Play
by Nastassja

We know more about the movement of celestial bodies
than about the soil underfoot.

—Leonardo da Vinci

CAST OF CHARACTERS

ESTELLA[1]: Our hero. Young scientist, pregnant, suffering from PTSD and hallucinations.

LEOPOLD[2]: Estella's boyfriend. Also plays SURVIVOR #1

WES[3]: Estella's father, a teacher by nature. Also plays SURVIVOR #2

DANCERS: Three dancers who will play each of these roles:
> TRIBE OF NEMATODES: Steampunk-dressed creatures of the underworld
> DIRT PEOPLE: Loin-clothed creatures of the dirt itself
> MYTH PEOPLE: Lakota, Sumerian, Greek, Japanese, and also play SURVIVOR #3

---

1   A tribute to Estella and Aldo Leopold, conservationists; developed what's now known as the Land Ethic

2   Aldo

3   A tribute to Wes Jackson, current soil scientist and farmer

AUTHORS NOTES

I imagine the tone of this play as steampunk, experimental—this is a *new* world order. Part of this will be fostered by the projections (which are an extension of Estella's mind and imagination), and thus the stage must have a large screen—perhaps fabric stitched together—which hangs in front of the cavernous back, which not only separates the lone survivors from the back room (thus trapping in heat), but is also useful for these projections, which could appear distorted on the uneven surface. They could be translucent, thereby allowing for back-lighting and silhouette effects for the dance scenes.

In Act 1, an underground bunker should be *suggested*, both in its cave-like grunginess and its claustrophobic conditions. An old staircase or ladder on one side leads to a suggested trap door. Roots (made of twine, etc.) are hanging in, low enough to touch. A bookcase, an old refrigerator, a mattress, and a bathtub are also tucked in this small space. Other attributes might include: darkness that is illuminated by flickering light via a generator on the fritz, failing hydroponics and light tubes, a light shaft, and a fan. There is evidence of long use, with rusted metal, dirt reclaiming walls, etc., but efforts have been made to keep it up and organized, particularly in the one small front room visible to the audience. There is scientific equipment on a table, kept clean and polished.

In Act 2, which occurs above ground in the same location, there's the suggestion of the remnants of whatever town this play is performed in (the director to adapt location and some of the lines to a specific locale), with burned-out trusses and crumbled buildings in the background. The fabric/screen remains and now serves as a way to project the moon, weather, and further footage. There are small spring grasses and dried-up winter grasses. The world has been destroyed and is slowly recovering.

ACT I

Scene 1
Setting: Cold underground bunker.

Rise: Dim and flickering light rises to filthy ESTELLA waking on a filthy mattress in filthy blankets. In the dark, we can make out LEOPOLD silently working at the science table, counting something.

ESTELLA: Oh, Leopold, what have we *done?* Leo, where are you? Leo?

LEOPOLD: Estella, we made a mistake—

ESTELLA: *(stands to go to him)* My god, I don't feel well. The body is no place to live. A baby. A baby into this? What were we thinking? *(holds him from behind)* Let's write that play today, let's—Hey! You're a lot hotter today. Forget the play, let's read up on home remedies—we gotta figure out what's—

LEOPOLD: [4] Tell me a tale of stem or stone…Tell me a tale other than this one…We made a mistake—

ESTELLA: *(leaning into him, lovingly)* A baby into this! Fucking breaks my heart. The audacity. To bring a soul from nonexistence into *this*…thresher. This thresher called existence. This thresher that chops up lives and hearts and hopes. We just created suffering that did not yet exist—

---

4   From James Joyce's *Finnegans Wake*, about the underground.

LEOPOLD: —about the food pellets—

ESTELLA: —Wait, what?—

LEOPOLD: We made two miscalculations. This *(puts his palm on her pregnant bump)* and the food pellets *(nods at food trays)*. Listen, winter is coming, and it should be snowing and storming up there, and listen, Estella. Listen to me. I'll need to tell you something—

ESTELLA: No, I'm not listening to you! You're going to say something crazy! Let's get up and do our thing! *(walks to front stage, determined)* The schedule begins—Breakfast! Brush teeth! Do the exercises! Read! Create! We must fill up our time. We must fill up our souls—

LEOPOLD: —Listen to me. Today I need you to listen to my story. Up there? I wonder if the snow is circling down gently today, spirals of mercy, sweet silent white, putting out the fires. Think of that, Estella! Isn't it beautiful? Our cheeks are rosy, we can see our breath—*(walks to her)* So pretentious. So audacious. For any human to assume they have much time. And yet, we all want more time, don't we? We assume it.

ESTELLA: We do—it's in our nature—*(looks queasy, retches to side)* Oh, god. I don't feel well—

LEOPOLD: —Morning sickness. The baby is taking root! Listen, Estella, sit. Sit with me. Think of all the storms, all of them, across all time and space. Storms of all varieties! Blizzards and windstorms and hurricanes and tornadoes and…dirt storms. There's one particular storm that holds in my mind today. I need you to listen to me

this one time, Estella. There was one storm. An Antarctic storm. Robert Scott, the explorer—

ESTELLA: *(retching, exhausted, sits back down)* I've heard the story,
  Leopold. Stop, please—

LEOPOLD: I *need* to tell it, Estella. Today is the day I need to
  tell it—

ESTELLA: *(ignoring him)* I don't feel well. The body is no place
  to live. It's like a prison cell. Tight and claustrophobic.
  Just like this place. Just like this planet. Remember when
  we used to *feel well?*

LEOPOLD: I need to tell you—

ESTELLA: And to bring a sweet creature to this misery…this
  thresher, this cave, this final exit!

LEOPOLD: *(gazes at the ladder/hatch, then stands and turns to speak
  loudly to the audience, as if gently lecturing, to make her listen)* Robert Scott left the tent. No, it was his lieutenant.
  On that Antarctic expedition. In 1911. On that race to
  the bottom of the earth. The man knew he was dying,
  knew he was a liability, there was a blizzard, and the
  others had a chance of survival. The Terra Nova expedition, it was called.

ESTELLA: Please stop—I'm so hungry it *hurts*—

LEOPOLD: Terra Nova. New land. "I am just going outside
  and may be some time," he said. In other accounts, he
  said, "Don't come looking for me, boys." *(checking equipment throughout the bunker)*—And he walked out into that

storm, knowing he'd die. And he did. A story of courage. Sacrifice. Duty. And maybe false bravado, because
no one really wants to do that—

ESTELLA: *(hissing)* I'm so sick of you. I hate you, I hate what
you did to my body, I'm so sick of living—*(hangs head)*
I don't mean any of that. No, I do. I—I'm going crazy
down here.

LEOPOLD: *(Walks over to the electrical box to tinker with the generator)*. It will get warmer now. Listen to me now, Estella.
Growing up with you here is the only thing that kept me
sane. You and your father and the rest of the Preppers.
We kept each other from going crazy, we did a good
job living down here, keeping a schedule, being good
to one another. But I want you to know, I would have
loved you if we'd met up there *(nodding up at hatch)*, if the
world was as it should have been—

ESTELLA: *(walks to the fridge and starts robotically pulling out breakfast, blocks of food of different colors)*. It's not right, to bring
a baby into this—

LEOPOLD: —A mistake. How many people have made this
same mistake throughout history? Millions. Billions—

ESTELLA: —But we bear the weight of knowing. We have foreknowledge. We know about the planet and what she can
no longer do—

LEOPOLD: —Yes, exactly, and so listen to me. While you slept
last night, I cut the hatch—

ESTELLA: *(startled)* No—That's not true—

LEOPOLD: *(satisfied with the equipment, grabs her shoulders firmly)* There, I just checked the generator. And last night, I checked the fan. And the tubes.

ESTELLA: No. You didn't.

LEOPOLD: I brought out the last of the food pellets. The aquaponic stuff is starting to fail. You might as well use up the compost spikes. Use everything up. Listen. It's mid-December. You'll be giving birth in April—if it goes well, if—

ESTELLA: Oh, no! Where you go, I go. You are *not* leaving me alone—

LEOPOLD: I'm going to die, Estella—

ESTELLA: You're not that sick—

LEOPOLD: I am. You know I am. And if you go up, you die too. It's too cold and there's likely nothing—nothing up there. You and the baby—*(touches her small belly and cocks his head, as if confused something could be in there)* I'll do what I can to leave you a shelter. Whatever I can find. I'll leave what I can, right up top.

ESTELLA: Who knows if she'll even—*(indicates baby bump)*

LEOPOLD: —Then just you *(produces gun slowly and carefully from his jacket)*. This is for you, Estella, in case that's true. We all need an out. Stay down here as long as you can. Daydream, daydream. It is the only war against reality, and this reality hurts. Daydream, and a backup plan. *(nods at the gun)*

ESTELLA: *(ducks her head, calms)* I should be crying. I know I should. Because I love you. And you're dying. But I can't feel anything anymore. I can't feel how sad I know I am. Does that make sense? I'm dead already, too.

LEOPOLD: *(holding her from behind, rocking her)* That's one thing I love about you. You're no coward. You don't live in denial. So many did. Thank you for your bravery. Please thank me for mine. Because I'm scared. I am sad. I can't do this without some sadness. But I'm tired and I'm nearly gone too. *(holding her hands to still her, holds her deeply)* Try to smile, Estella. I want to go up top and turn into dirt. It's like Whitman said: "I bequeath myself to the dirt to grow from the grass I love. / If you want me again, look for me under your boot soles."

ESTELLA: *(pulls away)* I don't *want* you in my boot soles—Listen, Leopold. *(grows seductive, to keep him)* We can portion off the food pellets. You're right, we'll test the dirt. When there are increases in the soil carbon…

LEOPOLD: *Debitum Naturae.* Our debt to nature is that if born, we have to die. And you're right. It's pure folly to assume a certain amount of time. Mine has come. *(looks her in the eye)* I just know it. *(rocking her, pointing to roots)* Think of it! I'll grow into a root and come down and visit you! It's winter up there now. Wait as long as you can, Estella. Wait till spring. Estella, daydream.

ESTELLA: Don't leave me *alone.*

LEOPOLD: You won't be alone. You have your mind. Your work. A creature kicking you from the *inside*! I'm going out and I may be a while. Terra nova. Terra nova…

ESTELLA: *(screaming)* Don't go. Do. not. leave. me!

LEOPOLD: *(jerks away, climbs ladder)* Let me go! Let me do it right. *(Throws back hatch to reveal a square of blinding light, howling wind. He turns back and must now shout to be heard.)* Estella! Listen to me! The snow? It looks like white bees. Buzzing. A simple miracle! *(looks around outside, looks back at her)* There's no sign of...I can't see...scorched earth... But it's moisture, beautiful white moisture. Write that play, Estella. Dream the play. Tell a better story—

ESTELLA: Please don't leave me. That's all I'm asking—I'll tell you a tale of stem and stone—

LEOPOLD: *(yelling)* Don't come after me, boys. To Terra Nova! *(clamor out, slams door)*

ESTELLA: *(primal scream)* My god oh my god I am all alone. No one knows me. When you die, there's nothing to miss, because no one really knew you. This has always been true: if no one knows you, then you are *no one*. *(Sinks to knees.)*

(BLACKOUT - END OF SCENE)

§

Nate! He leaves her. Now she's alone. And this part of the play is too long to send you, Nate, but what basically happens is that Estella starts to go cray-cray underground by herself and sometimes she talks to her baby bump and sometimes she daydreams up various people. Here are some examples.

Scene 4

ESTELLA: *(rouses self, starts gathering materials into a duffel bag)* I'll do what I can to leave this place as healthy as possible. In case it's needed again. *(looks up toward hatch)* I can always come back.

(Continues to put items in a duffel bag. Tentatively puts the gun in. She looks around one last time and takes a step toward the stairs. She is about to ascend when a major pang of labor hits. She doubles over. Screams, followed by a loud ping of the bunker creaking. She limps to the chair. Looks at the trap door, tries to rouse herself, but can't, sits back, and collapses into a chair. Makes a low, scared humming noise. She's terrified, but doesn't have the energy to leave yet.)

(Gazes at roots, panting) Baby Eva, *(pats baby bump)* I'm about to go up. Before I go, I'll show you your roots. *(gets out the camera)*

You know, there are no deep roots. Apparently, there were never any really deep roots. That people had to a place, I mean. Had to Earth. Or perhaps there were roots, just not enough? Or perhaps there were enough deep roots, but too many people? I don't know. But I do know this: When there are no roots, a thing moves. And moves. And moves. Wait, baby. I want to show you your roots. So you know from where you came.

(Stands, gingerly, and starts swinging the roots, filming them. Then points the camera at herself and speaks into it.)

My name is Estella. I am your mother. I don't want to die, but I might. Here is where I live. *(Pans bunker)* Here is what I eat, (*shows food pods*) here are my friends. (*shows hanging roots, considers one root lovingly, still filming*)

Listen, Baby Eva. I have to tell you one important thing about my father. One that tells something about me. It starts with Sartre. I think it was Sartre. He said, "Daydreams tell us to the extent we are not living."

See? We daydream about what we most want. When he was young, my father could only daydream about falling in love. Because, you see, that is what he lacked most in his life; that's what he most wanted. Then he fell in love and the daydreams stopped.

Later in life, he daydreamed of winning the lottery. Because he wanted to buy a farm, and what he most lacked was money.

And late in life, when my mother had died, and the farm had failed, his daydreams were all about him arguing with people. Because, he said, that's what he most lacked. He most lacked *justice*. Bad politicians got elected, people had the wrong priorities, and so he dreamed and dreamed of arguing, of fighting, because he felt so helpless. He lacked power to do anything about it. In his last days, down here, he daydreamed of the sunshine. Of budding trees. Of the smell of things growing. Because that's what he most lacked, and most wanted.

He would list them, there at the end. 'My daydreams were thus: Love. Money. Justice. Sunshine.'

I understand his daydreaming about arguing. It can be

good for us. There were so many fights. They'd even fight about what to call it. Soil! Dirt! Soil! Dirt! *(smiles)* My own mind argues all the time. I daydream all the time. You should know, Baby Eva, that some people tried. That the fighting was, in the end, perhaps very important…

(END OF SCENE)

Scene 5

GOOD PERSON: *(Angry. Looks in direction of the audience, as if he is speaking to the future.)* May the bad people live two days, starting yesterday.

Because they're leaving us without power to fix the problem we so clearly see. *(picks up old government book, picks up Bible, holds out each in each hand, shakes them, lectures audience)*

We, the people of this decade, are the ones who are witnesses to the end of one world and the beginning of another. I have come to believe that religion is for people who are afraid of hell. Spirituality is for people who have already been there. And stubbornness and the inability to change are sins and side effects of religion. Do you see? We confused ethics with religion.

Could it be that we are being obstructed in our desire to save the planet by those who believe in a god instead of ourselves? By politicians who need to be reelected? By governments that mortgaged our future? Religion, culture. Ego. Is it holding us back? *(points finger skyward)* Could it be that you *do* exist, and you're just devoted to monumental indifference? *(points finger at audience)* Your role in this is enormous!

The thing is, is that the Earth is shivering with the astonishing beauty of creativity, of human souls, and this beauty comes from fourteen billion years of creation, and now, right now, at this moment in time, we have to show ferocious love.

(BLACK OUT)

(END OF SCENE)

§

Nate, this is the end of the play. She's above ground now and has gone into labor:

SCENE THREE

From the audience area, the survivor group approaches. We start to hear the conversation below. It is playful—a competition of the best dirt quotes (trying to one-up one another). They come into view, a group of rag-tag survivors. Old backpacks or bags, covered in dirt, carry shovels and hoes. The survivors are all women because that's who should take over now. They are in an excited discussion of which we only hear fragments as they near. They do not yet see ESTELLA.

SURVIVOR #1: So, Chief Seattle said it well, and early. 1852. "We are part of the earth and it is part of us...What befalls the earth befalls all the sons of the earth." Ain't that the truth?

SURVIVOR #2: Leonardo da Vinci said: "We know more about

the movement of celestial bodies than about the soil underfoot." Ain't *that* the truth.

SURVIVOR #3: Aldo Leopold: "Land, then, is not merely soil; it is a fountain of energy flowing."

SURVIVOR: Wendell Berry: "The soil is the great connector of our lives. The *source* and *destination* of all."

SURVIVOR: Homer, from the Odyssey. I like his take: "I would rather be tied to the soil as a serf...than be king of all these dead and destroyed."

SURVIVOR: Rachel Carson: What a genius. "Those who contemplate the beauty of the earth find reserves of strength, which will endure as long as life lasts."

SURVIVOR: Aldo Leopold, I tell you! "We abuse land because we regard it as a commodity belonging to us. When we see land as a community to which *we* belong, we may begin to use it with love and respect."

SURVIVOR: I like the women best. Amy Seidl: "While it is relatively easy to recognize the perennial grasses and seed-eating sparrows as characteristic of meadows, eco-systems exist in their fullest sense *underground*."

SURVIVOR: "The nation that destroys its soil, destroys itself." That was Franklin Delano Roosevelt.

They all clap at him, acknowledging he's the winner of the quote contest.

SURVIVOR: *(walks to raised garden bed, holds up dirt) We* are doing better now. We have found our own wisdom now.

(THEY find ESTELLA who is getting closer to giving birth and like the wise men, they bring her gifts.)

SURVIVOR: A gift for the child: seeds.

SURVIVOR: Good gifts for the child: a trowel.

SURVIVOR: Real gifts for the future: a loaf of bread *(steps back)* We'll treat this baby like gold—

SURVIVOR: —by treating our dirt like gold.

ALL: To Terra Nova!

SURVIVOR: *(kneeling to pick up a handful of dirt, standing, and showing it to the audience)* Won't you?

SURVIVOR: *(kneeling to pick up a handful of dirt, and showing it to the audience)* Please?

SURVIVOR: *(kneeling to pick up handful of dirt, smears on face)* Do something today?

Stage black

Baby cry

END OF PLAY

Name the winds by Alexis

Straight Line Winds (those are dangerous fire-spreaders, tree knocker-overs)

The Ridge Roarer (when the fire spreads fast and mom's eyes dart to our go-bag)

The Back-and-Forther (the worst one, when it comes from all directions at once)

The Four Directions (all four directions, but they slowly rotate around)

The Ash Blasts (when the wind blows ash in my eyes)

The Howling Cow (which comes at night and sounds like a cow)

The Willy Willy (that's a real one from Australia, where my dad is from)

Chinook (winter when it gets warm)

The Burning Buck (when the horses gallop by and leave a wind)

The Quiet-Quiets Breeze (what I'm hoping for)

The Kiss (that will be when a boy's lips touch mine for the first time and I breathe out in a soft breath of happy)

Autumn's before & after

The snowstorm killed some birds. And some aspens. The birds froze and the aspen limbs snapped in the weight of snow.

Before that, Autumn had put up hummingbird feeders on the aspens. Believing, as she did, that depression was often lifted by acts of generosity. This wildfire had her feeling down, no doubt about it.

Before that, part of this wildfire sparked another wildfire, and they both raged day after day and now the blue Colorado sky was extra gray. Also, she had a black eye due to ash falling in her eye, then her rubbing it. That's all it took, oddly. Plus she had rashes and a chronic cough and bloody nose.

Before that, someone stole her BLM sign. Which she had to explain to her neighbor didn't stand for the Bureau of Land Management.

Before that, she went to the hardware store to get spray paint to make the BLM sign. She went with her daughter, who suggested they use the paint not for signs, but rather to graffiti the hate church on the county road. Because everyone was sick and tired of seeing the coal-rolling trucks with huge American flags, which had nothing to do with religion. This church was *nationally* famous for its hate. Autumn had laughed and said *no* and responded as a parent should to such a proposition. No, they would not engage in graffiti (parents often lied). While at the hardware store, she also bought a small chainsaw for pruning the trees on some future blue-sky day.

Before that, she had been secretly driving up to Wyoming to graffiti. Which, of course, she did not confess to her daughter, though she was shocked that genetics extended to acts of defiance. Her secret graffiti had started innocently. There was an enormous boulder in a field known to locals as Haystack Rock, which had been painted for years with happy birthdays or prom invitations but now had a swastika, so she went up after the daughter was asleep and took care of it with a PEACE, LOVE, BABY DUCKS. Haystack Rock was a turning point.

PART 2: AFTER

After that Haystack Rock endorphin release, she continued with her painting. She learned to be careful about wearing gloves to keep paint off the fingertips, and wearing masks because of shifting winds, and hiding her clothes in the back of the garage, because by then she was doing things no longer acceptable by law, although she felt ethically right in that she only painted places that were the worst-of-the-worst, such as the fence of the coal-rolling truck owner that she'd seen down at the Colorado hate church but whose owner lived in Laramie. Plus, she never-ever-*ever* painted something like stone or brick.

After that, she got better with the spray paint, and her increase in skill was directly correlated to her mood. The world got worse; her painting skills got better.

After that, she decided to tell her daughter the truth someday about survival and how one must keep doing positive things in the face of sorrow. Such as, the morning after a midnight trip to Laramie, she painted a THANKS FIREFIGHTERS sign and put it next to a new BLM sign but she made sure to use different colors and handwriting different from her Wyoming Escapades, as she had come to call them.

After that, the big snowstorm hit, which killed the birds and the aspens, but did not kill the fire. The wildfire continued on, strangely enough. She picked up the dead birds and buried them, chain-sawed up the aspens. It was one of the most depressing days of her life.

And after that, she took her chainsaw and more signage to the hate church. She put up a flag of planet earth, and a pride flag, and a random flag of national parks because she happened to have one. A sign that said KINDNESS WINS. She sat in a lawn chair with her chainsaw in her lap. Her daughter came with her. Then some others came and soon there was a crowd. They sat in the church parking lot for no other reason than it had come to this. The dudes in their big trucks with flags sat in the beds of their trucks and listened to country music and talked and she was surprised by the lack of heckling. They looked young and bored. Someone got out a guitar. The ash flittered down. The sky pounded gray. Her nose bled a little. But after that, she felt better, or, at least, good enough to go on.

the abandoned milk truck's graffiti

JESUS SAVE OUR PEACEFUL VALLEY
FROM THE DEVELOPER

NATE ♡ NASTASSJA

WE ♡ FIREFIGHTERS

THANK YOU FIREFIGHTERS

FREE
SHOWERS
KOFFEE
FOOD
AT THE CORNER

DEAR MAMA: EARTH WE'RE SORRY

Feather's eye

The psilocybin tea bloomed in her brain—Paige could tell because the golden cottonwood leaves were suddenly and enthusiastically clapping for her, but not only her—they were clapping for the sky which was blue today despite the wildfires, and they were even clapping for the helicopters, the ones with flying buckets drooping from them like peacock feathers filled with blue water to save homes, homes that people stayed in to save lives and stop viruses.

How good-hearted it was, for them to be clapping.

Indeed, that was the point—her particular nervous system was certainly and singularly freaked out but simultaneously not the center of the universe.

The helibucket was a feather's eye with blues melded with greens melded with a golden center, same shape as cottonwood leaves, same shape as her tear on her cheek—yes, a cliché tear—that signaled how very important this all was, this clapping, this feather.

Gretel's Solar Fire
Interpretations Report

CHART DETAILS

Gretel Kahne – Natal Chart
Feb 14, 1971, 3:05 pm, MST +7:00
Blue Sky, CO, 40°N35'07", 105°W05'02"
Geocentric Tropical Zodiac
Placidus Houses, Mean Node

Balance of Signs:
Scores: Aries 3; Taurus 1; Gemini 0; Cancer 3; Leo 0; Virgo
1; Libra 1; Scorpio 3; Sagittarius 4; Capricorn 2; Aquarius 5;
Pisces 0

Sagittarius strong
Inspiring, generous. Naw, she kind of doubted it. But who
wouldn't try to be generous in a time like this? Like, yesterday.
When she pretended not to see the sheriff setting up the barricade and motioning for her to turn around, and instead pretended obliviousness, skirted past him, and drove a bit too fast
up the narrow canyon to the home of the woman who had hit a
deer outside her house. She'd asked around about her—Korine
at the bar knew everything. Together they lugged a few of the
women's belongings out, and the woman introduced herself
as Mariana, and she introduced herself as Gretel, and admitted she'd caused the deer to run in the road, she was so sorry,
and they filled both their cars, and drove off the mountain just

before the sheriff's deputy would have forced them off, just before the helitanker dropped the sludge.

<u>Can be reckless</u>. Yes, true, like the time she plinked a deer with a BB gun and caused an accident in the first place.

<u>Can be tactless</u>. Yes, like the time she told Norman, who just did her Solar Fire Interpretations Report and printed it off at her house—his way of cheering up all the fire-evacuees, doing one for everyone—that this was all hogwash, disproved by a thousand different Snopes-type reputable science sources.

Also, like the time she got a dog for all the wrong reasons, which was today. She got the dog because it was running down the street, tagless, and so she brought it in, and it ran right up the stairs and jumped on Mariana, sleeping in the guest room. Now the terrier face with a shaggy mouth is looking at her all lovingly, and Mariana is making tea, all while the mountains burn up nearby. The wildfire is wreaking all sorts of havoc, including dogs running loose. And an elk—elk belong in the mountains, not at the base of the mountains!—is literally in her yard, chomping on her lilac trees. She can't believe it. She's never seen an elk at this elevation. But her eyes can see the evidence. She can't believe the Solar Fire Interpretations Report, because, well, it is not real.

Aquarius strong

<u>Humanitarian</u>. She did go get Mariana, after all. She did put up a sign that says FREE SHOWERS, COFFEE, FOOD for all the evacuees.

<u>Rebellious and eccentric</u>. So she told her up-mountain neighbor, Norman, who had done this Solar Fire Interpretations Report

(as a way of flirting with her, she now realizes), that she was indeed rebellious against what she perceived as a real danger in today's society: non-science masquerading as science. To her mind, the problem was basically this:

The practice of astrology and predicting one's fortune based on the positions of the sun and moon and planets and stars is quite complex in the way that cults and strange belief systems tend to be. This obfuscates and confuses people enough to convince them it's real, just like deep state and conspiracy theories. But fundamentally, astrology is at odds with the science of astronomy for one major reason: the dates of the zodiac.

Specifically, she told him, astrology suggests that each sign of the zodiac fits into a 30-degree slice of sky, which multiplied by 12 adds up to 360 degrees. But no. The constellations vary in shape and size, so, for example, the sun passes through the constellation Scorpio in just five days, but it takes 38 days to pass through Taurus, and so on. This is one reason astrological signs don't line up with the constellations of the zodiac etc. and etc. The *main* reason astrological signs fail to line up with the zodiac, though, is a wobble in the Earth's rotational axis. This is called precession.

And precession is a big deal. As a result of its rotation, the Earth bulges slightly at the equator. Kind of like how an ice skater's skirt fans out as she spins, she said. The gravity of the moon pulls on the bulge, the Earth wobbles, and this movement alters the view of the zodiac from Earth, making the constellations appear to slide to the east, isn't that cool?

So, like, in ancient times, she said, the vernal equinox was in Aries. Due to precession, it moved into Pisces around 100 BCE, where it will be till around 2700, when it will move into Aquarius.

Norman looked at her, then at his hands, and said, *we are talking two different belief systems here,* and she said, kindly, *astrology is like a game, and if it's treated as a game, that's fine. But it has no basis in science. It is to science what Monopoly is to the real estate market. It is like believing that the local sheriff will actually help you and is a good man. No, he's not; we have evidence to prove otherwise.*

Still, though, she likes looking up at the stars. Especially the black space between them.

BALANCE OF ELEMENTS

Scores: Fire 7; Earth 4; Air 6; Water 6

She does wish the Earth was in balance, yes. But: no, no, no, no. There is no way that her Fire outweighs her Earth. Her yoga teacher has already told her that she's way heavy on earth and lacks fire, in fact.

The dog wants to go for a walk. She and Mariana decided they'd name her Smokey Bear, in honor of the bad forest management that produced the drama that caused the dog to be here in the first place. And because the dog is smokey gray. She understands the dog's desire, but the sky is as thick with ash as it's ever been; if she leaves her home and the air purifier chugging away, she'll immediately get a headache, a bloody nose, and her eyes will itch. And Mariana is at work at the dairy.

This shit is real. No joke, she heard that the neighbor's best friend, a volunteer firefighter in New Mexico, was just diagnosed with lung cancer. He attributed it to the fires, so many of which are not just trees burning, but propane tanks and houses and chemicals of all sorts.

"Imagine that," she said to Smokey Bear. "Dying because of a good deed you did. Because of your *volunteer* work."

The dog panted in response, so she put on a mask and fashioned a collar out of a climbing rope and took him out, came back, cleaned her bloody nose, took a shower, and sat in front of the air purifier. She was pretty sure people on the East coast, such as her family, had no fucking idea how bad it was out here, and she irrationally hated them for it. Hated how the balance was off, and that Fire was indeed winning out over Earth.

Fire 7, Earth 4, yes indeed—that one did seem true.

BALANCE OF HOUSES

She thought having someone in her space would annoy the hell out of her, but so far, having Mariana in the house has indeed made it feel more balanced. She spends a lot less time in bed, for example. If only because it's embarrassing. Also, the kitchen is in better order.

She read her Solar Interpretations Report aloud to Smoky Bear, picking out her favorite exoteric and esoteric keywords:

biological inheritance,

artistic pursuits,

recreation,

children,

and lovers.

Smokey Bear raised one ear and panted. "Yes, that about covers it," she told him. "That would about cover it for any human."

What she needed—and needed bad—was a lover. She missed the wet zinging feeling between her legs. She knew arousal created wonder and well-being, when she felt akin to other creatures and the planet. Sex was like being on shrooms—very connected, very pure. For as long as she can remember, her body had gone through cycles of arousal on its own, and she was horny as hell now.

BALANCE OF QUADRANTS

She was 2ND QUADRANT STRONG, apparently, which meant she was receptive to other people and emotions. (This made her laugh because she had a history of wincing when people referred to themselves as 'empaths,' because, um, she wanted to tell them, I'm sorry to tell you, but most people are.)

Truly, no great receptiveness was needed here: neighbors evacuating during a wildfire produced a rather strong undercurrent of stress in the air. No one, not even a moron, could miss it. It was as if the air was charged not only with ash, but with stress, with a high-pitched scream of everyone's nervous system. She wasn't woo-woo, indeed, she had such a nice time making fun of what she considered to be a worldview equally as dangerous as all the stupid religions in the world. But anyone, even the most non-woo-woo among humans, could sense the energetic field in the air.

Maybe it was because she had stress and lust on her mind, but she felt the energy in the air was as obvious as the energy of two people meeting and being attracted to one another. Women's sexuality—her own, in particular, since that's what she knew—

was powerful, and the capacity for pleasure, the possibility of sequences of orgasm—well, it was a firestorm.

BALANCE OF HEMISPHERES

Scores: Eastern 3; Northern 11; Western 14; Southern 6

Western Strong

Supposedly, her interactions with other people take on a paramount role. Up to now, no, that had not been true. But now she had people camping in her yard, Mariana in her guest bedroom, and people coming in and out of her house to take showers. She was chopping vegetables and fruit at nearly all times. Her garden hose was continually on, as people filled their water tanks and storage containers.

One of these was Norman.

"Sorry I made fun of your...you know, belief system," she told him one day, standing outside the tent he'd pitched in her yard.

He smiled at her and caught her eye. "Do people have to believe the same thing?"

Her cheeks flushed. "Well, no. But it can be tough when there are really different world views."

He took a small step toward her and smiled. Flirting. Aggressively flirting. He too had had it with life. "When the world is as crazy as it is now," he said, "I can't imagine *any* view mattering all that much. As long as two good hearts are involved."

So she stepped forward and tilted her head up, put her hands in his dark hair, pulled his head down, and kissed him, and the kiss immediately went to lust, their hips pushing forward, into one another, with a force as strong and basic as wildfire. And they immediately push-pulled each other into her bedroom.

CHART POINTS

THE MOON IN SCORPIO

"You have an emotional intensity and a strong need for drama. Under stress, you will create drama and intensity in your life," Norman read from the astrology report, naked and in bed next to her, both of them still panting a little.

"I don't think so," she said. "Before the fire, I sat at home, alone, on most days, and just quietly did my work." Smokey Bear curled up on her lap.

ASPECTS OF THE MOON
SQUARE MERCURY

"You are indecisive, spending much time weighing up the pros and cons. You can be charming and pleasing in relationships," he read.

"Obviously," she said, running her hand down his chest straight to his again-hard cock. "Mariana will be home soon."

"Mariana. Good. I'll make dinner. And sandwiches for everyone outside. Lots of sandwiches."

"Deal."

"I can spend the night inside with you, here, on a bed?"

She laughed and poked him in the chest. "Ah, so that's why you want a lover. So you can have a bed."

He held her to him. "Naw. But sure is a nice side benefit." Then he kissed the top of her head. "Will you be my girlfriend?"

"We just met," she said.

"Even so."

OPPOSITION SATURN

She stayed in bed and read the next part to herself: "You feel abandoned and neglected by the loved ones in your life. No matter how hard you try you do not seem to be able to feel the warmth and caring that you need. As a young child, you may have lacked warmth and comfort from a parent figure."

"Naw," she said to the printed and now-crumpled papers of her Solar Fire Interpretations Report. Then she got up and dressed and went into the kitchen, where she could see the tent city in her yard. Out under the cottonwood, she watched Mariana laugh at something Norman said, as they both did some work of setting out food on the picnic table.

She bit her lip. Of course, she realized that's exactly what she had to sit with now. To not close off. Not shut down. To embrace this warmth and caring.

ASPECTS OF THE SUN
SQUARE NEPTUNE

The last paragraph, she had memorized. "You are a sensitive and soft person, apt to be overwhelmed by your empathy with suffering. You have martyr-like tendencies. It is time for you to leave behind your past inhibitions and truly express yourself in this lifetime. A major event will force you to come to express your fullest potential."

Okay, she thought. *Well, here it is.* The largest wildfire qualified, and the time was now. She took a big breath in. The air in the house was clear and she didn't cough. So she took another big breath in. Now Mariana was humming upstairs. Norman was outside visiting with the fire refugees in her yard. Smokey Bear was at her feet, looking up, tail thumping. Her crotch ached in a most wonderful way.

From the window, she could see Norman talking to a group of people and gesturing toward the house. They'd discussed this. Was the air too gross to have people camping outside? But was COVID too much of a threat to invite everyone inside? There was a vote: People preferred to sleep outside. But she still hauled out anything soft she could find. Bathmats, yoga mats, blankets, couch cushions. Sleeping pads got donated.

This sucks, this time just sucks for so many people, it's killing me, she thought, but she dug out an old Monopoly game and horse-shoes from the dusty garage. She was constantly putting on water for tea, and filling pitchers of ice water, some with sliced lemons and others with peppermint from her garden, after she washed the ash from them. Oddly, despite the trauma, she felt more energetic than she had in some time. She formulated the following belief system for herself: the body wants comfort and pleasure, the mind wants knowledge, the spirit wants peace, and often they're incompatible. But for this brief moment in time, they were not.

PLUTO IN VIRGO

That night, everyone formed a circle on their various pads and mats to look at the stars, because, briefly and happily, the smoke had cleared and the stars were visible.

"Pluto in Virgo, 1957 to 1972," Norman said to everyone. "Pluto takes 248 years to make a complete cycle, therefore, the interpretation of Pluto in its sign applies to a generation, not an individual."

"Hogwash," she said, reaching down to pet Smokey Bear. "Balderdash."

Norman put his arm around her and pulled her in tight. He was happy. "This generation possesses the ability to transform the way the world sees health," he pressed on. "Medical research, worldwide diseases, and the links between mind and body will be the focus for this generation. This generation may also have new concepts about justice. This is the generation which seeks new ways of achieving *right relations*."

"I shot a deer and it ran in the road and Mariana hit it. I feel horrible," she said, bowing her head.

"*Sí, y aquí todos estamos*, here we all are," Mariana said.

She looked up, breathed in. The stars hung bright. The Milky Way crossed the sky. The sky to the west glowed with red. Everyone was quiet. Norman had his arm around her. "Right relations," she said. "That's something in which I could believe."

Time Wedge

What's
happen-
ing here is
the narrow sec-
tion of what's called
the "Decisions Time
Wedge" and that's when
things happen really big and
really fast. Only time for reaction.
Very few options left and no time.
And those are very scary days.

Fire just passed the 200,000-acre mark. Evacuations. People are stressed. Put at risk. Values at
risk. Kay has died.

In wildfire land management, we have this wedge. In the
winter, say, we're at the fat part of the wedge, when there's lots.
of. time. to. slooooooowly consider options. And pause. Plan prescribed fires, do a NEPA analysis, ponder various responses. That's
when resource managers have time to think. A resource specialist such
as myself is to serve as a resource advisor, which means we help the
firefighters meet the law and policy. So whether it's me—a fisheries
biologist—or an archeologist or a soil scientist, we're trying to meet
standards of the Clean Water Act or historic preservation of archeol-
ogy sites. Law and policy. This is a beautiful, beautiful time.

Here's an analogy: If your house was on fire, and you called the fire
department, and they showed up ready to do their jobs, but first,
you tell them, Wait! make sure you watch out for the special stream

nearby, watch out for the old historic cabin over in the meadow! Of course, they're going to ask, "you want this fire out or not?" So, let's agree: in an emergency, such as this, with Kay dead and however many homes—we don't yet know—gone and smoldering, then yeah, when they're trying to deal with life and property being threatened, and time is of the essence, they don't have much time to care. This is a hard, hard time. A hard-for-everyone time. I feel for us all.

This
decision
wedge, of
course, applies
to climate change
and we better move
fast fast fast. Act, act, act.
Move, move, move.

For a while now, we've been in the
medium part of the wedge. We had time
to think. Study. Write reports. Hem and
haw. Have some debates. Instead of coming up
with a solid plan, we wasted this middle part of the
wedge. We wasted this time and it got worse. For example, now, Republicans have somehow formed the belief
that taking care of the planet is a liberal wacko thing (where
did those good Republicans *go*?) and there's no hope now of finding solutions.

That analogy of the firefighters showing up to put out the house fire? That applies here, too. Like, yeah, please put out my fire. But I also want to drive my SUV everywhere and have low food prices and remain apolitical. Or worse, I want to "Make America Great Again" by, ya know, keeping on with extraction, colonization, racism, degradation, and meanwhile, we are not putting out the fire. And the firefighters cannot do their jobs.

We have no fat wedge anymore. We are in the narrowest part of the Decisions Time Wedge.

The planet is burning.
We need to get the
fires out. Then we
can discuss other
stuff. Please. Pay
attention to
which part
of the
w e d g e
we're
in.

Naomi's calls on the Crisis Hotline

Dear Mama Earth,

Check out this postcard from the Rio Grande Gorge Bridge! You may know it as one of America's highest—650-feet drop, hard to imagine, I know, two football fields down!—but unless you've been a little person standing here, you wouldn't know how scary it is. Let me attest. I was standing up there, pre-Great Isolation, pre-wildfire, and for one thing, that's so far down to the Rio Grande River. Also, each passing car makes the bridge sway. Also, there's the history of suicides and thus the prevalence of telephones with signs CRISIS HOTLINE: THERE IS HOPE, MAKE THE CALL with encouraging stickers and graffiti. So, that's a lot of swaying scary stuff. Plus—you know me!—I was standing there with climate grief and democracy grief and things felt like they were falling apart, and there was this moment on the bridge when all I could think was, *This is a disgusting, rocking, queasy feeling!* That moment helped prepare me for this current queasy. Love, Naomi.

§

Hi Mama Earth,

I am imagining your reply to me, and yes, I did want to pick up that CRISIS HOTLINE phone, not because I was suicidal, but because I was curious. Who was on the other side? But I didn't want to bother anyone. Now I wish I had—that was my chance. To tell whoever answered about the crazy Taos-blue sky and the clouds and the view, and to say, "Look, I'll be honest here, I'm actually calling in planetary distress, and I can't kick this queasy feeling on this swaying bridge of life! Do *you* have anything to say about how to endure?"

§

Hi Gaia,

I wanted to send another photo of you, to you, this one taken in my backyard in Blue Sky, Colorado, with wildfire smoke blooming in the sky. They don't make postcards of these things—wildfire smoke—hence the photo. I wanted to tell you that I had a strange COVID dream, and in my dream, I picked up the CRISIS HOTLINE phone and you answered. You said right away, "I'm not going to answer with sweet platitudes about how great my sunsets are—although they are pretty great, right?" I agreed they were. Then I asked you for help, because things are pretty nutty around here these days. "I'm going to help by silent example," you said. "I am going to demonstrate how to bear witness, how to be resilient. Things are going to shit. It will be difficult! More swaying is to come! Sure, here's a gorgeous cloud. Mountain mahogany spirals are nice. But also, kid, look what damage can be done and yet some things still recover! Let me show you a list of some handy-dandy tips!" But then you hung up! I can't believe you speak so informally, Mother Nature, and also, your voice sounded raspy, as if you'd been a smoker all your life, but maybe that's the fires?

§

Dear Earthy Mom,

Suddenly I'm getting these mysterious postcards. One has appeared daily in my mailbox. My kid Alexis runs out to get them.

Postcard #1 said this:

Advice #1: PATTERNS. Nature is a balm and a solace—and boy, those are in short supply these days.

So start easy with repetitive things you've come to expect: birds migrating, leaves changing, early snows—I will offer you normalcy via the familiar. Each year, the house wrens return, the fawns slide from mothers, and the moon will be in phases. Learn where the birds nest. Notice those endlessly-changeable clouds and how they're sweetly lit as ever.

§

Postcard #2 said:

Advice #2: ATTENTION. Cultivate the right kind of attention and go from the superficial to the substantive. Become better seers. But it's not that easy. Being better seers isn't something that happens with the eyes. You can start there, sure, but it really has more to do with how you organize information in the brain. What is connected to what? As we know, attention is the most basic form of love. Did you know you can actually *learn* to love better? Remember this: hell is suffering from the incapacity to love, as you no doubt read in *The Brothers Karamazov*.

§

Postcard #3 was sloppily written and it took me a while to decipher:

Advice #3: MORTALITY SALIENCE. You people are on a rickety bridge that's swaying wildly with planetary and cultural and ethical dilemmas, and you know it, and knowing you can't get off the bridge is the tricky part! I know you all want solid footing, though you also know there's none to be had, and you wish you didn't always know it so fully! Process this mortality salience. Do not live in denial of death. Embrace the fact that things end, and you know they end, and that that is existentially hard, but it's also the natural order of things. There is no life without death.

§

Postcard #4 was clear:

Advice #4: RESILIENCE COMES VIA AMAZE-MENT. There are days when you will be amazed by people's generosity and selflessness, by the planet's resilience and beauty, by a gust of laughter, or a brook. Remember that river, so far below you, and be amazed! When the day has been hard, remember that the clouds boiling up over the mountains—they are requesting that you lighten up with them.

Advice #5: ACTION. Stop going for green chemical-infused lawns. Keep your cats inside (sorry). Conserve water. Conserve everything. Protect habitat. Plant good bushes. Get away from fossil fuels, fast. Split up into two countries if you need to, a great national peaceful divorce, so that some of you can move faster. Otherwise, you're going to dilly-dally around, bickering about stuff, while I burn. Think bigger. Much bigger. Much out-of-box-bigger.

§

Postcard #6 read:

Final advice: BE IN THIS ALONENESS TOGETHER. Scribble some helpful words in Sharpie on CRISIS HOTLINE phones for people, family and strangers alike. Metaphorically speaking, that is.

§

Dear Mother Earth of the Crisis Hotline,
I received six wonderful postcards from you and I thank

you. Here is one last postcard from me, again from the Rio Grande Gorge Bridge. I found it when I was cleaning out my house, which is what I do when I get antsy these days. Did I tell you? I was standing on that bridge because I was visiting Aldo Leopold's home right down the road, and thus had at least 1.5 million good-looking acres of trees around me for a month and I was in *this* America—this America of protected lands and in the home of a man who warned against consumption, reliance, the separation from nature and what it does to the soul. And that's when you started talking to me, I realize!

And did you know? This canyon was not carved by eons of erosion, like the Grand Canyon. No, this gorge was caused by one big rift. A big tear. If we attributed pain to the planet, we would think that was one mighty painful event, a crisis-like event! Was it difficult?

All I know is this: When the time is right, maybe this winter when the fires are over, I'll take my kid Alexis and go back to that bridge and stare down at the huge cavern. I'll pick up the phone. I'll say, "Hello?" and I'll hear your raspy voice saying, "CRISIS HOTLINE, MAMA GAIA SPEAKING," and I'll say, "Hey! It's Naomi and Alexis! What's that you said? Endure? And what else?" And you'll say, "If you listen, I have a coupla ideas on wise and humble rebuilding." And we'll tilt our ears down to the cavern and listen.

Love,
Naomi

Azura's unearthing

AZURA SPENDS TOO MUCH TIME AT THE ABANDONED CEME-
tery, and yes, she knows she ought to limit the time she spends
there because, yes, there's only so much that can be gained from
the past. But it's hard to resist the half-buried, lichen-encrusted
tombstones. The heart wants what it wants, and at this stage in
her life, and during such a catastrophe, she wants to give her
heart more of what it asks for.

Today she has gone too far; she knows it. The wildfire's
approach is forcing everyone to fit every last-bit-of-living in
while they can. She's working on an excuse if any passersby see
sher from the distant county roads, and yes, that could happen,
since the old cemetery rests on the south side of her ranch,
the side nearest the new subdivision that is nestled, with her,
in these foothills of the Rocky Mountains. It's entirely likely
that someone might notice a middle-aged woman in jeans and a
white tank-top and ponytailed gray hair standing near the largest
tombstone with a shovel in her hand. Surely they might wonder,
but she hopes any curiosity remains buried—she just doesn't
have the energy to explain why she's digging up earth in search
of a lost soul. Nor, frankly, would they want to see the body
she's about to unearth.

§

Azura has forgotten how much pain a body can hold—she
hasn't felt this much hurt since the birth of her son decades ago.
Her arm muscles ache, her hands are covered with blisters, her

stomach muscles throb from lifting the shovel. She wipes the sweat from the side of her face with her forearm and feels the skin stretch on her bare shoulders, tight with sunburn. She's put a pebble in her mouth to ward off thirst, and she rolls it around on her tongue and meanwhile coaxes herself: *Think of Arapahoe setting up community, think pioneers crossing plains, think French trappers tired, think of all who have loved this place, even if they did it wrong or incompletely, press on, press on.*

At least there was the brief rain. Certainly not enough to put out the wildfire, but enough to make the sage sing with smell, the yucca and mountain mahogany gleam, and there's something about the tangy wet soil, of life, and, although this seems crazy, there seems to be a hum of gratitude from the earth itself. She's often thought about how the ground offers a gift in return for water, the earth's curious ability to spit up treasures after a rain: arrowheads, glass bottles, bits of crockery. Water falls, and the earth offers up.

§

The shovel thuds against wood. Something electrical surges through her chest with such force that her body sways back from the impact, and she drops the shovel and walks away. She wants to hold on to this moment, to let the thrill take hold.

There is a small bench she has brought for visitors to the cemetery, and she eases herself down onto it and surveys the tumble of land before her. Here are the lives lost to stillbirths, scarlet fever, whooping cough, typhoid, suicide. One hundred and seven people are buried here, all the early settlers in the region. And before that, according to the stories, it was a burial ground for the Arapahoe and Cheyenne. There's so much she wants to learn, wishes she knew, people she would have liked to observe or speak to. She has written a book, one that took years of research—a slow process of unearthing stories, piecing together information. The book is not a morbid necrology, she writes in her introduction, but a celebration of ordinary lives. Because of her, none of the dead are just initials or names any longer. The barely visible, clumsily-engraved letters have new meanings. She likes to think that because of her, their lives have been somewhat resurrected.

She looks at the stones of these people she's been laboring for. When her own time comes to join them, she knows there won't be much time to peruse the possibilities for the best last thoughts. She is prepared. She ticks off the list of things to say to herself in that last moment of life: First, it will be "Oh!"—or some sort of yelp of surprise—and then, "Damn!"—because of course she'll be furious—and then, "I'm scared." The next part she says to herself over and over as she examines the land in front of her. "Shhh, shhh, don't worry. Think of healthy mountains. Think of how the heart feels on a hot summer day," she whispers, and then, "Goodbye to the soul of Azura."

Probably it is ridiculous, this rehearsal. But she has learned about the importance of a proper goodbye, and she wants to give herself what she can of a comforting farewell.

§

Since Azura first discovered the grave of Alphonse Morrisette, she has been holding long conversations with him in her mind. His was the very first burial recorded in the county—1878—certainly, he was not the first burial, of course, but the first recorded burial that she knows of and they share French descent. She figures there's a lot of catching up to do. She has explained what cars are and how they run. She tells him what housing developments are and why they all look alike, about the world's current population and The 'Vid or 'Rona, as she alternately hears it called, and about new farm technologies and the current price of cattle. And wildfires. Megafires. She tells him of the New West, how poor, or just regular, or even medium-wealthy landowners are getting forced out, how Subarus have replaced pickups and fleece has replaced wool. She tells him about his French trapper father and his Oglala Sioux mother, Mary, or, more beautifully, White Owl, and how, after Custer, she was forced to move to Pine Ridge. She acknowledges his surprise at things such as computers and planes—she explains how they work and when they came into being. He'd be surprised that she wears pants, that she has control over her life—women's rights, Azura thinks, are a true paradigm shift, whereas a virus would be more understandable. She argues with Alphonse about the changes she perceives as good but which she imagines he has trouble digesting ("it was wrong of you to think that women were not your equal") and sympathizes with him regarding the changes that are clearly wrong ("yes, look at that foothill, covered with smoke—doesn't it make your heart break?").

She supposes others have these conversations with people of the past. But she wonders if anyone is as dedicated to them as she. She has an obsession with this man for reasons she cannot quite pin down. Perhaps because her farmhouse is built on the remnants of his log cabin. Perhaps because she occasionally finds old glass bottles, nails, handmade tools that she knows were his. Perhaps because she's lonely and crazy. In any case, she knows that such a strong curiosity is some people's definition of love. If that's so, then she has loved Alphonse for quite some time.

She rolls the pebble around in her mouth and gazes at the hill of gray tombstones and the waves of blue mountains rising behind them. A stretch of meadow spreads out where her Hereford-Angus cattle graze, a blue heron flies above the line of cottonwoods that border the river, the horses stand in the vee of a fence corner flipping their tails against the flies. And above that, a mushroom cloud puffs and spews gray hell.

It's true—Alphonse Morrisette and she have, by whatever bit of fortune, found themselves on the most glorious place on earth. Though their present state is not one which either prefers—he being dead and she about to lose everything and the world burning—she supposes that the sheer beauty of their current location should cause them to feel awed and at peace.

That's what they have in common, she and Alphonse. They have shared this bit of earth. He died in the process of defending it for his family. She, on the other hand, is going to let it go. But before she sells the small ranch, she's going to tell this man goodbye, a moment she will not be cheated of again.

§

She's so thirsty, but she doesn't want to stop now—she's too close. All she needs to do is pry the boards loose. She's on her hands and knees with the crowbar, and the timber is thicker and darker than she imagined it would be, and as she fights with the rotten wood, she pleads with herself: *Try not to be bitter. Try not to be sad.* She reminds herself that when she was young, she balked at the audacity of the old, who complained about their failing health, their forced relocations, their trials, their pain of having to lose what they loved most. How dare they complain, those who had been given the chance, the honor, the gift, of living an entire lifetime?

All hogwash, she realizes now. The old must see things whittled away, and in certain deep ways, that is no honor or gift. The body, the memory, the land—diminishing. She imagines, even, the mountains are being eaten away. But still, she tells herself not to utter a word of sorrow tomorrow, when she signs the papers. Five million dollars for two hundred acres in these foothills of the Rocky Mountains.

A developer has drawn up plans for all but the cemetery, which will, he assures her, of course, remain an important historical site. Azura has written her son, who wrote her a postcard: "Sounds good to me. You'll be rich!"

Her heart cracked a bit when she read it. She was hoping he'd argue, plead, get down on his knees and say, "Once this land is developed, it will never be the same. Cement sidewalks will take the place of the paths I took down to the river, fishing pole in one hand and a coffee can of worms in the other. The gravel road, with its snake of grass in the middle, will be asphalt. Houses with those godawful garages eclipsing the entrance will sit where the ground has never been tilled, since the first roots took hold there. Doesn't she understand the value of a place? How it is worth so much more than money, which is a figment of the imagination?"

In her imagination, he tells her how he will come home, and how working together, they will save the ranch. He will have knowledge that her husband didn't, he in his old, sweat-stained ballcap, squinting at a computer screen and tapping away at the keyboard with those beat-up hands of his, trying to figure out futures and options and a way to save the place. Who, like a fool, believed up until the end that they'd continue living in the old rambling farmhouse, continue checking on cows and selling fresh eggs and cutting hay. Maybe it would have worked, she thinks, if from nothing else, the sheer force of his will. It's just that on his way to check a pregnant heifer last March, his heart stopped too early. And he fell to the ground and died, before she ever got to tell him goodbye.

In her imagination, her son comes back to pick up where her husband left off. In her mind, such a thing is possible. Because in her daydreams, her son knows about the cows, that they must be fed, checked, doctored, birthed, weaned. He knows about the weeds that need to be killed, fields irrigated, trees watered, fences mended, about the garden that needs tending and the apple trees pruned, that the pump needs to be fixed, about the meetings to attend, taxes to pay, books to balance, cattle to sell. He knows that this is too much for a single aging woman, and he will fiercely battle for her and for the place, and he knows that although it makes for a humble existence that the land is worth it because this place is a beautiful place, and it is a place to belong to. Even when she knows there's no chance of such a dream coming true, she likes to imagine the possibilities.

And anyway, why not let the land be developed? A few more people will enjoy the view; perhaps someone will even appreciate it as much as she does. These new homesteaders will have their own smaller parcels of glory.

Besides, she did what she could, didn't she? This past year, she searched high and low for a buyer who would ranch the land, or for someone who'd keep it intact and safe. In the end, there were too many taxes, not enough money, nobody interested. So she settled for protecting eighty acres of open space around the cemetery. That's something, isn't it? Perhaps not enough, but God knows she tried.

She pushes her weight down on the crowbar. She's going to let it all go, with as much goodwill as she can muster.

§

Azura's breath contorts with the effort of something at the cusp of her ability. She pauses to cuss at the crowbar and ashy sky and starts again. Finally, wood splinters, and with more prying and pushing and gasping, she's able to move a thick board to the side. The moment it shifts, the smell of wood mixed with something like wet wool rolls out at her, and although there is no movement, she imagines the newly released air floating past her. She catches her breath because, for an instant, she is afraid of it entering her body. Mold or virus or death.

Then she exhales all her own pent-up air, pushing it toward the skeleton that has just come into view. She shakes herself, trying to clear away the prickles in her neck and spine.

What she sees is hair, black hair, coarse and wiry.

It hangs from a skeleton face.

A cheek is caved in on one side.

She leans back, then crouches forward again to pry off a second board. Now the skeleton is in full view. She feels as if she should pause, but she cannot wait to touch him. She leans and fingers the black hair, then moves her hand to the place above the right ear, where the skull is broken, clearly caved in.

Here it is, the wound that killed him.

She reaches out to touch it. Tangible and real and glorious. She runs her finger along the place that caused the end of a young life, proving the microfiche newspaper accounts of it true, and therefore proving all her research true, her hobby, and her fascination valid. But more than that: here is the *exact place* where life was taken, and perhaps in touching it her body will absorb his loss in a way that newspaper accounts and diaries will not allow her to do.

When she takes her hand away, she is startled to see what looks like a flake of dried blood on her finger. That can't be, can it? She looks at the dark, wispy fleck, the essence of Alphonse Morrisette. She wishes she could make it turn to liquid and flow again. There is so much she'd like to share with him. She would like to hear his voice speak whatever was last in his mind and see his eyes drift across their land.

§

She reaches into the coffin and lifts out his skull. She only has to twist it a bit to free it from the spot where it has rested for so long. She holds it in front of her. Part of the cheekbone on one side is caved in, and the bone is cracked and dusty. But the jaw is intact. And all that hair—she can't get over how long it is—it's not what she imagined at all.

"I shouldn't be doing this," she says at last.

The sun pulses down strange light from its afternoon position, hanging above the smoke-covered mountains. Helicopters drone to the West. Sirens rise from the mountains. Azura ducks her head a bit, the movement of a person being accused, to deflect judgment. As she does, a shard from the skull's cheekbone falls to the ground. She watches it settle among the rocks and dirt.

"I suppose you'd like to know what hit you." Her voice is just a whisper, so she clears her throat and starts again, louder. "First you were walking home on a cold March night, and the next thing you knew was darkness. Did you know you were dying? Did you have a chance to tell yourself goodbye?"

She looks past the skull to the rest of the body. This man was quite tall, just as she'd assumed. The legs are covered with leather pants, cut narrow, and fit like jeans. The leather is surprisingly soft and clean. There are no boots—this doesn't surprise her, since she knows shoes were so valuable they often weren't left on the body. Brown wool socks cover the feet, though, and through the material, she can feel the crumbled bones of his toes. There's also a short leather jacket with wide lapels over his torso and arm bones.

She doesn't know what she expected, but she didn't expect this—to find him so intact, still clothed, after more than a hundred years. How can it be that he's still so much in the form of a human body, so close to being able to sit up and laugh and hold a conversation?

It takes some time before she can speak again, but when she does, her words rush out in a torrent. "Let me tell you about your last night. I read your cousin Minnie's diary. She said you'd gotten in a fight, defending your mother's Native blood, defending your family's right to stay on the property. The Custer thing had happened and all the French-Indian families left in 1878, first to Red Cloud and then to Pine Ridge, you sent your wife off, but you didn't go. I bet the old timers didn't care, but maybe one of the new settlers did. You left a bar one night and before you got home, an ax had been plunged into your head. You'd been talking about the mountains, the good river bottomland, said you were going to plant an orchard, said you were going to be the richest fellow in town. Said you were going to protect this place from all the condos, forty-acre ranchettes, strip malls that were to come. Okay, well, you didn't say that. I'm making that part up. But apparently, you said enough. Because on the way home, whomever you'd been bragging to whacked you with an ax." After a moment, she mumbles: "I'm sorry. It's a terrible way to die, when you don't see what's coming." She pictures him falling, falling, his head ricocheting slightly off the ground. If only she could have been there to hold his head in her lap.

"I'm sorry your land is gone. It got parceled off and sold over the years. I own the last coupla hundred acres. Have you heard any of my conversations to you? I have to move away now because at some point, a person just has to give in. I'm sorry to let you down about that, but it's complicated. There are taxes and debt and now wildfire and I just don't want to die, I guess, in the attempt to hold it together. Plus, my son doesn't want to live here. This place meant sacrifice. My husband and I loved it for that, but my son hated it for the same reason, and all he remembers is the duct-tape on his shoes. I keep telling myself that sacrifice must be kept in check, or it becomes the ruin of souls. Isn't that right, Alphonse?"

She considers the skull, which she has put on the ground beside her. "You had some passion for this earth. We would have walked it together, across the deer trails," she says. "Or, no, probably we would have hated each other—because I can see where you might be a tough bastard, a hard man—but who knows, maybe we would have been happy. We're both a bit ornery, a bit odd, a bit dreamy, aren't we Alphonse, aren't we?"

His jawbone looks like it might be smiling. She wonders if he enjoys feeling the warm mountain air, which still has undercurrents of cool from the rain. "My husband and I used to walk the land together, too, looking for arrowheads. Bottles and tools. Perhaps you were the person who touched them last, before me. That makes us not so distant after all, doesn't it? It's funny in how certain ways time can be collapsed." She runs her finger across the leather above where his heart once beat.

She hears a rustle nearby and jerks her head up, but it is only a meadowlark flying out from some foxtail grass. She looks down the valley at her white farmhouse and the cottonwoods clustered around it. There is the beat-up pickup, her peacock fanning his tail in the reflection of an old bathroom mirror she'd left out for him, chickens wandering around the yard. Nothing special—only her life.

§

Near sunset, she picks up the skull again and puts it back in the coffin and smooths the coarse hair from the flat bone of the forehead. His skull tilts to one side a bit, and some of the black hairs rise up in the breeze. "So, your life. Now it's all a bland piece of history. My life will be the same, of course. All that drama and joy and pain ends up as a newspaper blurb. We all get reduced, smoothed over. I did what I could to keep that from happening, but I think it helped only a little." She feels the sting of tears rising, and wipes at her eyes with a forearm that smells of salty sweat and dirt. "This was my last cockamamie search for a lost soul, Alphonse. Goodbye."

She stands up, brushes the dirt from her jeans, and begins to replace the boards, stepping on them to press them tight. Then she picks up the shovel to move the dirt back in. Evening is on its way, full of deep blues, and she watches the color shift and darken across mountain and sky. The sirens and helicopters have called it a night. All is quiet. As she works, the speech she used to give during her tours of the cemetery runs through her mind. She tries to stop it, but there it is anyway, circling: "There are certain things to be learned from what has come before, and this is what I believe to be true—

"One, the past happened.

"Two, it can't be recovered.

"Three, but archaeology can be done, and it can be done

well. There will be gaps, of course, there will be gaps, but really, there's no alternative. History and its archives, archaeology and its artifacts. It has to be enough."

She always ended with this teacherly list. Then she would add: "We can dig into the past, and discover the limitations, or we can not do it. I choose to do it." She repeated this last bit with what she hoped to be an air of grand finality. Even now, in her mind and with no audience at all, she punctuates these last words.

Well, today she has accomplished what she set out to do, which is to verify that the limitations might be too damn great. That's all she needed to know. And so now she'll try to end her conversations with this dead man and try to remember how much earth separates them all. When she forgets this, she will think of how cool the earth smells when dug up, how smooth it feels in her rough hand, and how it looks when a shovel slices through it.

She spits the pebble into the hole, onto one of the dark boards, and fills the shovel, intending to cover the coffin with earth. But instead, she steps onto the board, onto Alphonse, intending to send them all down, farther away. She pays attention, but there's no apparent evidence of her force. The wood does not crack, the ground does not shift. There is only the sensation of something moving up her leg bones, some divulgence that the earth always wanted to spit up things, always wanted to grant access, always wanted to give.

Sleeping on the hill as retold by Ty

I AM HOLDING THE SKULL OF A BLACK-HAIRED GUY IN MY hand, and he's lit by my flashlight, and the crickets are chirping, and it's spooky as hell. He was buried in the 1870s in the old pioneer cemetery that rests on the hill. The hill is where everyone is going to watch the fire. Which is where I was when I saw Azura standing, talking to a mound of dirt—she'd just re-buried this guy—so I went to stand and talk to her. Knowing, as I do, that she's all alone, as so many of us seem to be. I gave her my copy of *Braiding Sweetgrass* by Robin Wall Kimmerer. I quoted her this section about fire: "Touch it here in a small dab and you've made a green meadow for elk; a light scatter there burns off the brush so the oaks make more acorns. Stipple it under the canopy and it thins the stand to prevent catastrophic fire."

She snorted. Because catastrophic fire is what we now have. We didn't listen. To those sleeping on the hill.

Before this was this cemetery, it was a Native burial ground. And now it's dark and everyone has gone home to supper and finally cooled off and I've come back. I had, after all, been reading my *Spoon River Anthology*. I've considered teaching it next year. And I thought, all these souls sleeping, sleeping on the hill, none of these graves have epitaphs, and no one speaks for them. I took it as a sign that I just happened to be reading Edgar Lee Masters when I came across Azura, who, like Masters, was trying to let the dead speak.

Obviously, she's feeling a little insane, as we all are. People do weird things when they're under duress. So she reburied him, and since the soil is still unpacked, I've dug him up myself. I'll put him right back. I just wanted to hear what he had to say, too.

My breath is calming—moving soil takes effort—so now I can really take a look at this guy. He has a skull that's caved in on one side. His teeth are creepy. But creepiest of all is this tangle of matted, dirt-filled hair. It's just so…human. He was alive not that long ago.

I am familiar enough with life and familiar enough with death and know also that this is messed up. But I just have to do it. So I say, "Here's your chance, what do *you* wanna say?"

Silence.

Dang. Looking at the rest of him is weird, too. Headless man in remnants of a leather jacket, leather pants, some old-looking socks, a tumble of toe bones—all of which I see by my cellphone's flashlight. I turn it off and sit down on the grass, next to his body and hold his skull in my lap and sit next to the pit that holds the rest of him and we just sit in the dark, stars and moon shining overhead.

I sigh. I'll be this guy soon enough.

I wonder what *my* epitaph will be. I wonder what I'm going to say to myself when *I* die. Probably I'll be surprised, then pissed, and then, I hope, I'll have enough time to get calm and peaceful. To do that, I'll imagine this valley from this cemetery hill.

Then I hear him loud and clear.

"Oh, I hear you! I know what you are saying," I say to the skull.

I do as he requests: I stand up on the hill and hold his head up as far as I can, arm outstretched to the sky, and even get on tippy-toes. I want him to have the best view.

I rotate him a little so that his eye sockets are pointed in the direction of the valley.

There are the barn lights on at Azura's place, and little dots of light across the valley, and the glow of wildfire to the west.

The air is smoky but cooling. It's rather quiet, save for a distant plane and the rustle of something over by the ditch. I give him plenty of time. I'm sure there's a lot he'd love to see. I recite bits of poetry. I tell him, "All, all, are sleeping, sleeping, sleeping on the hill."

I'm the Zone Duty Officer

Directions for Aerial Delivery of Fire Retardant:

Prior to aerial application of fire retardant, the pilot will make a "dry run" to find waterways. And then, when flying over these mapped waterways or riparian vegetation, the pilot terminates the application of retardant approximately 300 feet before reaching the waterway and waits one second before applying retardant again.

But mistakes happen, and when they do, fire personnel must immediately report the incident. Dispatch will call the Zone Duty Officer. Which is me. All those people not in the news, we're working hard, too.

I'll tell ya three things: one, water is sacred. Two, we are making mistakes. Three, we can applaud the firefighters, who do hard and excellent work. But at the same time—because we are adults with sophisticated thinking skills—we can realize we can do things better. I know we are trying. We are the zone duty officers of our lives.

Korine's acknowledgment
of White Owl's power

La porte. French for "the door" or "the gate" and that's exactly what this place is. Because this is the last meadow at the base of the mountains, with a river that runs through it, and that river provides a gate up into the mountains. *Comprenez-vous?* We modern folk may not realize how hard mountains are to get *into*, with our roads, but imagine. Imagine what it was like to try to get into these peaks. You needed a door.

I work at that door, at the bar (used to be called *saloon*) at the base of the mountain, and imagine that, a bartender/waitress such as myself loving history. Oh, the assumptions people make about a 20-something pregnant blonde.

And now, as the fire line creeps closer, with winds gusting the burning glow our way, we stand in the streets of Laporte. People up the mountain are fleeing here, to our door. When a fire is in your home, you are supposed to shut the door, no? So we welcome them in but also set our sprinklers—the fire must hold here. We are *la porte* that will hold the fire.

§

He-hos-ko-wea, or *White Owl,* also known as *Mary.* Sioux. I want to admit that I might get her story wrong but I've tried to do research and I want to acknowledge her life. Story has it she was sold by her brother to a French trapper when she was sixteen. I think of her often. I try to picture her face. I know she walked the river's edges, as I do. I wonder about the trauma of her people, the trauma of her individual life, and it fucking messes me up. Not *that* long ago, she was an individual with all her singularity, feelings, importance, in a time of tumult. As we are now.

If I could collapse time, I'd ask her questions that are maybe dumb. How'd she appreciate going from a beautiful name with a clear image—a white owl—to *Mary*? Did it clank in her mind? And did the words "marriage" and "Mary" go together somehow for her—because in marriage, she became Mary? And how was that for her? Not good, I assume? Because no one wants their land taken, wants to be *sold*. And how did it hurt in her heart?

§

Cache la Poudre means "hide the powder." That's the name of this river. The stories they tell kids (particularly in fifth grade, since that's when you have to take Colorado history) is this: in one story, a caravan of trappers and travelers were attacked, and they needed to bury their powder. In another, the travelers simply needed to lighten the load. In either case, legend has it, they buried their extra guns and gunpowder somewhere around here, and we locals have been looking for that cache ever since. And looking for the truth.

Look, I know not everyone is interested in history. Indeed, I myself am not. But something about having the future change right in front of your eyes makes you consider time—these mountains will not be the same in our lifetimes. Future Marys and Johns will see different mountains because of today.

So please, I want to say this, it feels very important to me:

I do not know what the Arapahoe, Ute, Cheyenne, Lakota called this place. I'm sorry I don't know and am not able to pronounce it correctly even if I did. That seems ridiculously dumb. I'm embarrassed.

All I know is that the French name stuck, *Laporte*, next to the *Cache la Poudre River*, on the banks of which lived *White Owl*,

who had a name in her own language that was even more beautiful.

§

The French trappers who came from Fort Laramie in 1859
founded a town that they called Colona, and later Laporte.
Then: Custer's "battle" (AKA *massacre*): June 25, 1876.

After the slaughter, and a slaughter it was, General Sherman
was given the power to assume military control of all reservations and to treat Indigenous people as prisoners of war. At the
same time, settlers were increasing in the valley. Pressure at the
door. Nearly every French-Indian family left and went first to
Red Cloud, Nebraska, then to Pine Ridge, South Dakota. White
Owl left. I think of White Owl, walking along the banks of the
river on the day she was forced to leave.

§

I grew up in the house that White Owl once lived in. Or, rather,
in the same location, since the farmhouse I grew up in was built
on their home. According to the *1894 Collins Express Special
Industrial Edition*:

> a few yards down the stream from the bridge, stand two
> log houses, one large and set back a distance from the
> road…the smaller one almost reachable from the back
> of a horse is the oldest house in the Cache la Poudre
> valley.

Yes, I know that spot.
It is my spot. And also their spot. All our spots.
So one thing I know for sure is this: White Owl walked the
same earth I do, hiked to the same ridges, had the same mountain views. Her family ran a ferry across the river, ran a saloon

in a log building with dirt floors, were the first to bury their children on a hill that became the historic cemetery where my own ashes will be scattered. I want to acknowledge her. I want to remember what I cannot know.

§

I wish White Owl and Jean Baptiste could see this blackened sky, the ash falling down, not because I want to make them sad, but because I want to commune with the past and future people of this place. I want to collapse time. I want to hug future inhabitants and past inhabitants. The gusts of wind, glow of fire make me want to commune with *all* the beautiful souls who have loved and walked this valley. Without speaking of it, we have all etched this exact place—this door—into and around our lives.

§

So I just ask that you know this: Where the river tumbles out of the mountains, slows its pace, spreads out—there is Laporte. Before that, according to photos and my imagination, there was a meadow of teepees. The most ancient evidence, according to archeologists, is the blind—a small rock outcropping built by human hands for hunting. Sure, the river course has changed a bit, as it should, and water levels are significantly lower year-round, now that water is diverted upstream, which is a shame. And now the mountains will be black. And then they will regrow. But you can see what I'm saying: not that much has changed. Our souls are all connected here. This place has power.

La porte. The door to the mountains. The gates to powerful forces. It is a vortex of love.

Here's what I hope: that some future person will walk through town and feel a little *amour du lieu*. She'll know of fire restoration, of better ways of living. She might circle around and come to rest. She might wonder about who came before and who loved it, too. She might wonder about heritage and history and stories. About old knowledge and local knowledge and the power of that. She'll think of *He-hos-ko-wea*. And she will feel she *belongs*. She will see that when the sun sets, the water in the river sparkles, the grass takes on a reddish hue, a blue heron flies to an outcrop of rock. And she will hear a phone ring, a child laugh, and she'll be aware of this place as a door to the beyond.

Dear friends I wish I had (from Sherm),

How ya doin'? Me, not so great. I just dug around my dusty cupboards and found a box of dusty tea and added a small dash of whiskey from my non-dusty bottle, though it's early in the day. It's because I have five sore throats in my one sore throat. Razor blades in the throat. Hurts to swallow water. Hurts to eat. Hurts to talk, which is why I'm writing. Haven't written a letter in years. Maybe decades. Maybe since my mom made me write thank you cards forty years ago.

I have The 'Vid again. Twenty days in and so not contagious but feeling lousy. I have already had it and there has been so much fog in my brain for so long. I am so tired. I am about to crack. I just butchered a deer, a wildfire is raging, I can't breathe.

I don't have those tests because they are nearly twenty bucks at the grocery. But I got my free government-issue two in the mail (stupid waste of money, if you ask me, but that doesn't mean I won't take advantage) and had to find my reading glasses to figure that mess out and sure enough, two lines. I'm feeling raspy in my lungs and last night I went from chills to burn, burn to chills. Sheets wet with sweat. So. I'm scared.

Hard to be sick alone. I could stop breathing and no one would notice. But even more, I could really use someone—wearing a mask of course, which I concede I made fun of—bringing me soup. Or just putting a hand to forehead. I'm watching a mallard duck take off, his wings flapping crazy as he skims along the ditch, and it seems like he'll never gain altitude, which is how

I feel. Finally, the duck cuts a better angle, rises. But other than the duck, when my eyes drift around, I feel like I can't *place* any of it. I feel like there's someplace in the fog I know will be clear, if only I can find it, but for the moment, I do not know really where I am or what I am doing on this planet earth, or who I am, even. In a way, it's terrifying, and in a way, I feel relieved that I know nothing and there's nothing to be known and I don't seem to need to know nothing.

Besides my lungs, there's another thing pressing. There's a phrase for it, I hadn't heard before listening to the radio in my truck. *Food insecurity.* And I had one of those moments, where like my brain connected that phrase with my reality. Like, whoa, there's a name for my condition.

Even if I hung my head and went to the community food cabinet, there would be only a few cans of beans, although I will grab those, and if I drove further into town, into the real food bank, I'd need the gas to get there and back (and I ain't going to ask them to deliver. And even if I did, they wouldn't, because the sheriff is only letting up residents, due to the wildfire and all).

I've got a roadkill deer, butchered and frozen. I eat a lot of dandelion greens and wild asparagus that grows near the ditch. There are apples that will soon be ready, assuming they don't burn. So I ain't going to *die* or something, but a person could sometimes use a little more than venison. I'd really like some carrots. And blueberries. An orange. A cake.

I guess I feel broke. My throat hurts like a motherfucker, my eyes have itched all summer, and it's hot as hell.

I ate the last of the canned soup yesterday, assuming my body could use some nutrition. The hot tea helps. I do have honey. Everyone else is voluntarily evacuated and most of them are camping down at that house on the corner, so I could, in a pinch, break into their homes and grab some food. I'd own up to it and apologize, of course. When I feel better, I'll go get a trout from the river. There are some things I can do. But I don't know how to make friends. So as to have someone here to say, *hey, man, I'm sorry your throat feels like that. What's that, you cracked your rib coughing? Oh, man, those hurt! Let me bring you a popsicle like you had as a kid. Let me check on you for just this one moment in time. Because fever, fire, and no food—those things surely feel scary, whether you name them or not.*

I have nothing to lose. I don't even have you. So I'm heading down the mountain. I'm crying uncle. I need some people. I need help.

Thanks, friends, for listening, I sure do appreciate,

Sherm

what I would have asked you

LAST NIGHT IS THIS: MAY I, PAIGE, COME IN YOUR TENT, Sherm? Curl beside you? You, who surprised me by showing up at our community tent city suddenly? Together conjure that power of a first kiss? Or have we, in our middle age, come to the place where we only note the stirrings of our bodies? Aware, as we are, of the troubles that such desires bring? Or have we gotten to such a place of exhaustion—viruses and wildfires—that we no longer have any bandwidth for desire?

As I listened to you put away your harmonica, which you had been playing pretty badly in the dark far away from the others but still lulling us to sleep and helping us forget the wildfires, I tried out phrasing for such questions, and I listened for any noise you, across the lawn, might now make. Me, single and lonely, you, single and lonely. Me, having just really talked to you, though you've been my neighbor for a while now. You, a grumpy loner. Me, a grumpy loner. My guess is we share some politics leaning a little right in the sense we just wish the government would shut the fuck up about most everything and get it together, yet also simultaneously wish that we ourselves could get it together a little more. Me, pulling the sleeping bag to my chin, you, likely sprawling on top of yours, hands folded at your chest as you regarded the night sky. The both of us evacuated along with others, various tents dotted across Gretel's lawn.

My ears ached with listening. The zing of crickets. The chilling of the earth and the deepening of the sky. I heard the murmurings of others as they got settled, including one loud bark of laughter. I listened to the most simple things, such as my pulse and breath, because, of course, love is a way of knowing, a way of looking at the ordinary until it becomes special and looking at the wondrous until it becomes common. Desire both amplifies and reduces our lives.

My breath was biting me like the stars bite the sky.

I hoped you would come to me, that I would hear your footfall, but I was also willing to come to you once I got the phrasing right, but the correct combination of words eluded me. Only a few syllables, really, but the basic question implied so many others. For starters, would you want to sandpaper off the edges of our skin that keep us so separate? What a question to burden you with, with others nearby! How were you to respond kindly, if the answer was no? And if the answer were yes, well, then there were others: do you have any STDs or condoms? What constitutes the basic theology of your sex life? How quiet can you be?

Since I, Paige, could not figure out how to ask you, Sherm, all that, I got up. I tiptoed to the place where we'd seen a rattlesnake at dinner. It must have been close to midnight, and by the light of the moon, I saw an apple sitting out on the battered picnic table, next to the empty bottles of wine. I felt like leaving a note, William Carlos Williams style: *Forgive me, but I am hungry in more ways than one, and this fruit was available and delicious.*

So, this is just to say, as I sit writing in a journal, witnessing our ecotone, where various species meet, that I wish I'd asked you the old cliché question, that same one humans have been asking one another beneath the star-spattered sky forever: what else is there, exactly, except for love? Why is it that we want to curl up next to someone so badly? Is there any way we can come together? In more ways than one?

Had you invited me into your tent on the outskirts of the lawn, beneath that large cottonwood tree, and had we made love, perhaps we would have curled like grapevines and spoken a great deal and slept very little. Nonsense would have ruled, as it always does when such feelings are allowed to surface. We would have unlocked mischief and we would have felt like we'd gotten away with something—an extra slice of life, for instance. We would have discussed much: past loves, future empty space, how hard it is to go for long times without sincere and rousing touch, how we might be fuck-ups. Life is lonely: on that, we would have agreed. Relationships are tricky: dwindling kindnesses, the inevitable and immutable taking-for-granted diminutions. Even the relationship we have with ourselves. We humans have not progressed so far in this regard; perhaps, even, we have gotten worse at sincere connections.

Last night, when the apple was finished, I walked back to my tent. Halfway there, I stumbled over something and fell and rose up, gasping so as to absorb the pain. It hurt so very much. There was nothing to do but bear it. Let it dissipate. When I was back in my sleeping bag, I jammed my jacket under my head and I considered Cassiopeia, visible from my screened tent window, and I formed words to try to ask you. I made little 'w's' with my lips, trying out sounds. I did hear little murmurings and sighs from one tent over and that's when I decided, finally, to merely walk to your tent and say your name, with a question mark attached. Or perhaps I would have said: lovers are in the hurt business, to be sure—but do you feel any urgency, do you think you'll live to be a hundred? Wake up and live with me, for just a moment!

But I did not. I became afraid. Afraid you would be sleepy. Afraid you would be unkind. Afraid that you saw nothing in me worth loving. Afraid of the old story, which is that last night, when I looked up at the moon, which was at its apogee, tears flew into my eyes because I was conscious that my life, too, is at its apex and that like the moon, my life is floating, ready to change direction, and I am afraid of growing old, and I am afraid that the deep and raging hungers of the flesh are perhaps too much with me, and yet it has been some time since I have been desired.

I am not sorry I ate that last apple in the moonlight because it was good and my mouth needed consoling. But I am sorry I never found the words to ask you one question in particular, one that I thought that maybe, just maybe, you'd have the answer to: given my silence, how is it that the remainder of my life won't only be a series of sad dreams and appetites that will occupy me, night by night, until my questions are gone?

On the topic of Mikaela and milkweed

MY SON NATE RECENTLY LOST HIS VIRGINITY, THOUGH HE'S quick to tell me that that's a patriarchal term and that not all experiences fit into the heteronormative view of sex, but that, yes, he did have what he considers his first real moment, and that it was great. He tells me this on our usual walk around the dirt road that loops our neighborhood in the mountains. He got the condoms at Planned Parenthood down in town, so thank god for that. He knows my reservations and rules, which are four:

1) no disease and 2) no pregnancy—both hurt the body;
3) no being unkind or 4) untrue—both hurt the heart.

He knows that I wish he were a year or two older, but he also hears the uncertainty in my voice about that one. It's possible we're all gonna die of COVID or fire. I just want him to be centered and calm enough to enter into a beautiful thing with grace, to which he says, "Mikaela-Mom, I appreciate that, but I *am* a teenager, full of raging hormones." He pats me on the shoulder. "But we broke up last week. Staj's family's cabin burned," and I tell him I'm sorry, and then we talk of Kay-who-died, the dead moose they found right near her body, the likelihood of our house burning down next, the fact that our mountain, Sleeping Bear, burned down to the scree and river, which makes us feel at least temporarily safe, and how the evacuation orders have lifted now that the fire has shifted south and west. Then we talk about his math homework and the fact that one of his friends has lice, because, that's the thing about life—it just keeps going haphazardly on, even in crisis and in love and in loss.

§

"Can we take a moment to relate to each other's feelings? Really *talk*?" He said this to me nearly nightly starting at age eight, and I'd curl up next to him and say, "Sure, but I'm guessing you just want me to stay longer, and I'm pretty tired," and he'd launch anyway into the emotions of his life—friends gone wrong, embarrassments and slights, his love for a girl he hadn't yet spoken to—all of which I took seriously because it was serious to him, and as I rose to go, he never failed to ask me, "Well, so, how's *your* heart?"

"Gup-Gup," I'd say. "You've been my best teacher."

And he'd say: "I hope you always call me your little gup-gup."

§

Now, he's seventeen. Has a '73 Mustang—cars are not something he knows about, nor do I, and my only hope is that it will be out of the driveway when he leaves for college. He's gotten drunk once and kissed a stranger on an airplane once and now he's had sex. "Ma, let's go on a walk," he says to me today, code for the wish to talk. Again we wander around Sleeping Bear Circle.

A helicopter flies slow with its big sling of water. We stop to watch a deer and the milkweed fluff and listen for a last canyon wren and he tells me of his ex-girlfriend. He tells me who is smoking pot, who is drinking, who is cutting. He gets into some very specific sexual questions and I laugh, plug my ears. I was, as he knows, raised Catholic, conservative, and harshly, and have spent a lifetime trying to grow in the opposite direction, and so we laugh about my limits. My heart feels—yes, let me be sentimental—as light as that milkweed, as bright as sunlight.

We might be forced to leave again soon. We've already taken important stuff to my sister's, and our Go Bags are packed here. But we might as well stay while we can, I figure. We might as well check on our neighbors' houses, including Nova, who is in Italy, and Bob the Younger, who never feels well, and who is now staying down at Gretel's place.

§

A time or two, I wanted to leave Nate, especially after his father died. Too much work, too many of my dreams deferred, too many times of getting up in the middle of the night. "Think hard before you have children," I tell my childless friends when they ask. "No one warns you adequately." Exhaustion. I could say the word a thousand times and never get to the depth of how it felt to wake up on the floor, papers I needed to grade scattered around me, a child suckling on my breast, my eyes and heart stinging, my heart feeling cold and dead not because I didn't love him but because I was so tired.

§

It is, of course, the small things. The first time Nate brought me coffee in bed. It was six a.m., he was seven, and his face registered the difficulty of balance. The coffee had milk in it, and he'd heated it in the microwave, and my sleepy brain understood many things, such as how hard it was to open our microwave, how hard it was to pull down a gallon of milk, how I never said, but he must have observed, that I like my coffee hotter than the coffeepot could get it.

Moments of grace.

§

While I was having my second miscarriage, my body bleeding and expelling tissue, I walked to a state fair. This is back when I lived in the Midwest. I made it, finally, to the butterfly tent and stood inside, watching chrysalises attached to the netting. I stood still and watched, even when a cramp sent me gasping, because I wanted to see one born. It took much longer than I thought it would. I also thought the butterfly would fly off, bright and alive, but it didn't. It clung to the remnants of the chrysalis, resting, the wings slick with magic liquid, exhausted.

Nate will be out of the house soon. Flying bright. College brochures reproduce on the counter. I'm glad for it. Not only that he is launching, which was always my job, but also because I always had my own flight pattern.

§

The older I get, the more I believe we should be far more careful with ourselves than most of us generally are. I have lost so many people these last years, all middle-aged and all because of stress and this harsh world—lost them to mental illness, breakdowns, alcoholism, disease, death. Including my husband. All I know is this: had I not seen that butterfly being born at that moment, at the moment a could-be child was slipping from me, I knew even then, even as it was happening, that if I did not witness some sort of wonder, that something essential and tender in me was going to float away like ash.

§

When Nate was little, we'd walk around this loop, and he'd pick cattails and let out the fluff. It was on one of those walks that I felt, for the first time, the sensation of not-exhausted love rushing up my throat; pure physical sensation. How very aware I was that I needed to hold on to that moment, to be careful with joy.

I remember: a red-blond boy running ahead, fast and sure of himself in that ridiculous way children run when they're still wearing diapers and have puffy material between their legs. "Oh!" I'd said, surprised, and clung to it. I think I even said it aloud: "Hang on to it, hang on to it."

§

"Gup-gup," I tell Nate every once in a while, "you were my first teacher."

I do not say: sometimes it feels like parenting nearly broke the childlike, sexy, joyful qualities in me, but it's all okay now. You, now returning home from school, walking into the house in a moment, full of grumpy hunger and annoyance. Your summer has been a shitty wildfire and virus and now it's going on fall and the fire is still burning. We are about as honest and loving and tender as humans can probably get with one another, and that is so rare and lucky that I think I will crack.

§

Now he is asleep and I sit on the deck, absorbing the night. From here, I cannot see the glow of fire, but I drove up the canyon until I got to the barricade, so I could see how far it had progressed, then I drove home. The non-running Mustang sits in the driveway, the slobbery dog sits at my feet. I look up at the stars. I always look for Cassiopeia. When he was young, Nate would say: "Actually, mama, you actually smell like twinkle-twinkle little star," and I would say, "Thank you. I didn't know I smelled that way. You sure like the word 'actually.'" And he would say, "Actually, I do, mama," and he'd add, "Everyone's starshine should shine pretty bright."

One, two, three,
and a white junker car

Six problems I had the afternoon my brother called from his home in Laramie:

1. A wildfire approaching my home, which is all I got— besides my white junker car.
2. My dick hurt—a little patch had been rubbed raw on the left side by too much vigorous activity.
3. Crystal had unexpectedly started her period and bled through onto my mattress during the night, the first night she's spent over, and it's not the blood that bothered me, but something else—that I felt wholly incomplete, having to remember that basic fact about women. Stunning, the ways in which I don't seem to be aware of other people's experiences. There she was cramping and bleeding, whether awake or asleep I don't know, and I just slept through, oblivious.
4. My income from horseshoeing that month was $1,342 and my expenses were $8,900, given that my septic tank had just gone bad.
5. Given that fact, I was considering illegally shooting an elk for the meat this winter, because simple fear will do that to a person who is scared, and who cares anyway, they're likely to die by fire.
6. It's hot and windy as fuck. I have never wished for win-

ter but I do now. If it's not covered in smoke, the sun is beating down on us like it wants to fry us.

And then my brother. A simple buzz of the phone, changing everything. Informing me that:

1. His cancer had spread.
2. I needed to come get his daughter—my niece—ASAP, for the weekend.
3. Who else was going to adopt her if I didn't, huh?
4. I needed to get a better car—my white junker wasn't safe for a child.

My first thought, which was selfish and ungenerous, was:

1. That will mess up my date with Crystal.

My second thought, also ungenerous, was:

2. He can't die. Because that leaves his daughter parent-less, and that means major catastrophe for me.

It's possible I am a prosocial psychopath, a term I've heard used for people who judge every event, every piece of knowledge, based on how it conveniences or inconveniences them. Although I don't think so. I'm just a regular human, and don't they do that, too?

Finally, my moral compass kicked in, and I had a reasonable thought, which happened while I was staring at Crystal's blood on the mattress, me having stripped the sheets because I was heading into town anyway. That's when the phone machine (yes, I still have one; there's no cell service up on this mountain) started playing my brother's voice and he was whispering into my future. All I could do is simultaneously think: see, this blood is evidence that Crystal was going through this whole thing of blood and cramps and some sort of uncomfortableness while I was oblivious; and, here was my brother, his cancer getting worse, one worse diagnosis after another; and, here I am, having sex with Crystal while a young girl's only parent dies; which means, I am in a matrix of stupidity, a Möbius loop of oblivion.

The brain is a hard thing to unpack.

To describe.

Because simultaneous to all *this*—and all that was simultaneous itself—but on top of all this, was a low and dull roar of sorrow. Because life is simply harder than we think it will be. And that's sad. And I'm mortal. Death is sad beyond belief. It's that simple. And sad.

My brother, meanwhile, hung up the phone but was likely sitting right next to it, in his Laramie home, waiting for a response. About the future of his daughter. And I was staring at blood, trying to find something true about how my own blood beats.

§

I'll admit that the wildfire and my brother's impending death are doing a real number on me. I ran into a neighbor, Ty, at the laundromat, and Ty confessed to having had panic attacks for most of his life, since his teenage years. He's a sturdy fifth grade teacher who teaches Colorado history and who deals with preteens because he also coaches over at the middle school, and thus carries himself like he knows himself and knows the world. You wouldn't think he was capable of having a weak moment. He also tears up pretty easily. This, I have always been jealous of. I'd like to get one damn tear out per year. But the panic attacks—no thanks.

So, first I find a girlfriend, then my brother starts to die. All this affects my present, and a large scope of my future, but worse, a thorough examination of myself. Which is why I probably had my first panic attack. I wouldn't have even known what it was—I would have assumed I was dying—except for Ty's description. Which did not exactly match mine, but was close enough for some extrapolation.

Here's how the attack felt to me:

1. The world went black, then red, then black again.
2. My lungs cascaded down into my feet, totally devoid of air. I literally had no lungs in my chest. I know that sounds impossible, but if you would have asked me to point to my lungs right then, I would have been clawing at my kneecaps or thereabouts, sure that they had sunk that low.
3. Some kind of strong worm-like creatures must live in me somewhere—and I know we are all full of viruses and parasites and perhaps undiscovered worms, too— but this felt like a monster that swept up my throat and started strangling me from the inside. Right around the windpipe.
4. Not being able to breathe made my heart beat like it was in its last sprint, about to collapse, which is what I did, right onto the floor.

Now, what I should have done is call Crystal. That is what a relationship is for.

Or called Ty, or stopped by that lady's house on the corner who is offering free coffee.

But frankly, I don't know how to do that. I don't know how to have a relationship. I have never *had* an honest, long-term, real relationship. I never saw them modeled to me, nor have I figured out how to do it on my own. I mean this literally. My mother, who certainly did a pretty good job considering her own demons, had no long-term friendships so I could see what friendships looked like.

There were many things I did not get from my mother except her toughness, her ability to keep going, her ability to purse her lips, duck her head, and plow forward, and her white car, which is what got me through that panic attack. I kept saying what she used to say to me, which was *it's as easy as 1 2 3, easy-peasy, as easy as 1 2 3* and I breathed. One. Two. Three.

One. Two. Three.

I thought: It's not something they teach in school. How to—what do we even call it?—build community. Foster friendships. Care and be cared about. But anyway, after the worst of it had passed, I started thinking about Crystal and sex, of course. I thought it might calm me, and it did. Here is my list of things I thought about:

1. She likes getting drunk and acting on her sloppier impulses, which in sex means that everything flows a little crazier and more unpredictably. Sometimes I'm even a bit scared.
2. Her pubic hair is dark and unshaven and very curly.
3. Her nose gets red after sex—sex rash, she calls it—and she looks younger, more alive, more overcome by the capabilities of her body. Also, a bit like a clown.
4. Sometimes, in the right mood, she likes rough behavior.
5. Her fingernails are ragged and bitten. She sometimes stares at them, after sex, as if surprised by their existence. Or their raggedness. I'm not sure.
6. The way she focuses the power of her mind reminds me of a horse galloping, free of rider.

I stayed curled up on the floor in the fetal position, counting. One. Two. Three. I felt like I could sense a piece of good in me, but just then it was not available to me.

Grace, grace, I kept thinking, where are you?

I didn't call my brother back. I did have the feeling, though, that if I counted hard enough, curled up on the floor like that, perhaps I could find a piece of good in me in there somewhere.

I'll make the call. I'll take the niece. I'd ask Crystal if, in all her humanity, she might want to be my partner in it all. I'd rub some ointment on my dick. I'll drive to Laramie tomorrow afternoon and I'll try to drive slower. One, two, three things at a time, I'll try to distance the obliviousness that hovers.

Hell is empty

IN FRONT OF ME IS THE BAR, AROUND ME ARE TIRED FIRE-fighters and evacuees, and to my left is Sherm, who says he's over COVID but I keep my mask on anyway (lowering it for drinks, which keeps me busy) and since it's warm all the doors are propped open for this very reason. Sherm won't stop talking. Like a firehouse has been let loose. Never heard much from him—or most of the other neighbors—and now this. Can't keep anyone quiet. Suddenly we all know each other, and in this case, too well. So I keep my eyes on the lines of bottles with the shoulders drunk out of them. Shades of blues and greens and golds. Me, I'm drunk on the clears. Beautiful.

And beautiful pregnant Korine keeps them coming and sometimes offers intelligent observations about this place, its past, present, or future. (I say she is beautiful not because I'm a creeper or objectifying her in any way, but because she is, in fact, a beautiful human being on the inside, that's what I mean by beautiful.)

Sherm (who is unbeautiful) offers unintelligent observations. Right now, he is saying such nonsense as: Ty, that surge in deployment of troops in Iraq was one more attempt to keep American's attention off of the basics of 9/11. Ty, here's a fact: it's still an unexplained fact that the thing with five sides...

He pauses, and in the pause, my chronicle of emotional reactions goes thus:

Gratitude: that I am not him

Relief:	that school has been canceled so I can get drunk
Relief:	that no parents or school kids of mine are here so I can get drunk
Relief:	that soon I will pass out
Trepidation:	what if I don't?
Self-imposed relaxation attempt:	chill, man, breathe.
Waffling:	maybe I should go
Surprise:	Korine, pregnant, is bringing me another gin, having seen the look on my face
My voice:	the Pentagon? Is that what you mean?

Sherm says, yeah, I couldn't think of the word, my brain is all fried with this fire, but yeah, the *Pentagon* is protected by a huge number of the fastest and most accurate air defense missiles in existence and it is simply *unthinkable* that not a single defensive measure was taken. It's not *resolved*. We need to have a serious conversation in this country. We have free speech but not frank speech.

My eyes drift to the taxidermied animals nailed to the wall, then to the fake fish that periodically wags its tail, mounted to the wall above them. Suddenly they are the most interesting things I've ever seen. I chomp on a fried cheese stick.

Says Sherm: I bet our houses are gone.

Says me: it's possible.

Says Sherm: I got a bunch of venison in the freezer. Hope the electricity isn't out for long. What a waste.

Says me: a lot in life is a waste.

Sherm chomps a cheese stick from my plate and says: I think I'm capable of shooting up a bunch of people. Why? Because this world has too many of them. And it would be a gift. There's going to be a civil war if we don't get rid of some evil-doers. This is an experiment. For the next ten minutes, we'll say the most awful true stuff we have to say. Mine is that I feel like shooting people to rid the world of about one-third of its population. And I have no friends.

I snort. Then, says me: Sherm, you can't go shooting people. Killing them because they disagree with your worldview.

He says: you want to know what my crazy brother told me once? Before he was on meds? This was a few years ago. He told me that God fucked him in the ass. Literally. Then, to make up for it, God turned into a woman, a beautiful woman, and they made love. But still, God had made a mistake, and so promised to do one more thing for him. So my brother asked to see Hell. And God took him there. And it was empty. Empty!

I say, what did it look like?

Sherm says, empty. Big empty cavern with a fire going. Stalagmites and all. So it won't matter if I kill some people.

I'm gonna punch you, I tell him.

Okay, but listen, Ty. Let us begin with two assumptions. First, let us assume that George Bush was not nearly as dumb as he acted. Molly Ivins knew him in high school back in Texas, and she agrees that he is not a stupid man. Consider that the Boeing 757 of Flight 77 was possibly not the craft to hit the Pentagon—

I am going to punch you soon. I'm sorry I'm not doing it now—I'm just too drunk—but I'm going to do it soon.

—Six reinforced, load-bearing walls ruptured and the only way that could be explained is…well, see, the wing sections of the 757 would be sheared off entering the wall, which would leave only the aluminum fuselage—which is light stuff—to travel through the remaining five walls. From a structural engineering point of view, this is manifestly impossible. It was not an aircraft, it was a missile.

I beg the bottles: please. Shut him up.

I beg the animals: make him die.

I beg myself: don't wish death upon people.

Then, because everyone else is, we both turn and look out the bar's window and open doors. Rain is suddenly coming down, or rather, sideways, as if Earth has tilted. Rain! It's swishing into the bar by itself and also being blown in by the wind. No one gets up to shut any doors; it's too glorious. Korine is in front of me, looking at it, too, and her face has the look of someone who has just seen God.

Hey Ty, she says. Ty the teacher.

Rain, I say.

She smiles and winks and when she's gone to get a drink for someone down-bar, Sherm rubs his head and says, I'm a sick fuck. This has been a good little community. All in all. Despite the liberal fucks, such as you. Somehow we all manage to get along.

I pause. Set down my glass. Turn to face him. But Hell was empty, you say?

He blinks at me. Huge empty caverns. Cleared out. Stalagmites, stalactites, the whole bit. Fires burning, a bad smell, dark and dank. Smelled like fire. Like, it was all set up for people. But not a soul there.

my child will come as you depart

CAN WE *PLEASE* BE HONEST? NOT ALL OLD PEOPLE ARE NICE, I have learned, and not all grandchildren are sorry when grandparents die. I won't be. According to Marvin, Black people are lazy, women are sluts, liberals are nuts, and everyone at the care facility is a fuck. I told him he deserves a very hot Hell after he dies and that I won't be taking him on any more car trips. And that I don't know where his racism and hatred come from and that it confuses me but that it is clearly there and *that's* what's fucked. He throws his dirty Kleenex out the car; just tosses it right out to blow about among the trees, and tells me I'm a pregnant whore who only knows how to pour people drinks and why'd I change my name to Korine anyway, that's stupid. As he rolls up the window, he complains about the goddamn government, who should be taking better care of him and yet is also too big. Also, they're a bunch of faggots. They probably started this wildfire. He deserves more.

You deserve, I'd like to say, to pick up trash alongside the road, tugging your oxygen tank behind. You deserve to get down on your knees in front of most everyone and ask for their forgiveness. You deserve to ask the planet for forgiveness—you and many in your generation. You deserve to suffer because you didn't plan for this. The government doesn't need to put you up in a top-notch home instead of the crappy one you're in. They owe you nothing. I owe you nothing. You were supposed to take care of your goddamn self, save up some money, get good health care. You should have quit smoking ten years ago or else you should shut up about your coughing now.

I would say: this world just doesn't need you in it. There's enough of us already, too many of us, in fact, and some of us need to get off this planet, including you. To make up for the occasional sweet child, who needs the space and room.

Can we be honest for a minute? Doctors do us a grave disservice by keeping everyone alive. Some people need to die. Humans need to *die*, that is part of the deal of living. And here they are prolonging life at all costs because of their oath to not cause harm—well, docs, what about the rest of us? You think you're not causing harm to us? The ones who get stuck caretaking? The babies that will have a shit planet because of all this medical equipment and waste keeping old mean people alive?

The nurses restrain him at night, which is when he gets the worst. "We're not going to put up with inappropriate behavior," they tell me. I say, "Good. Fine. You don't need this in your lives." They're already dealing with Mrs. Hass in the hall, who screams for help constantly in the hour after her medication wears off and before she's allowed more. They have to deal with Mr. Rose starting up the Star-Spangled Banner each mealtime. They have to deal with the fear of dying; with the shit and spittle of living; and they sure don't need my grandfather adding to it with his "goddamn Mexican nurse can't you give me my medicine and if you don't get me out of here right now I'm going to smack you silly, stupid fucking nurses, all of you," and throwing his water pitcher across the room.

I am the only one who visits. His own children, including my mother, shut him out of their lives long ago. I can easily imagine why, though she never said much about it. I can imagine his belt sliding out from the rings in his jeans, I can imagine his hard fists, I can imagine his enormous body threatening, backing them into a kitchen corner. This man deserves to die alone; he does not deserve more time.

Not like my father, who did die alone, who needed more time. But we all know that life's not fair. There's no use complaining about it. That's what I tell grandpa now. I also tell him about waitressing and bartending, about the kid Alexis, and how I met Sherm and Ty, newly evacuees and therefore new at the restaurant, since they'd usually go to the one up-mountain, and then I tell him he's staying in that home, there's no money to move him, and he better leave the nurses alone. Then, just to get one dig in, I tell him that if he hasn't noticed, my baby will be arriving quite soon and my priority will be with the baby.

He rages against the seatbelt and suddenly I'm terrified; he's going to kill me while I'm driving, that he'll reach over and grab the steering wheel. I see his fists clench and unclench and he spits out words at me, that I'm a goddamn loser of a kid with a stupid name—Korine—pregnant and with no future, bet I can't even name the father, what a whore, what a whore.

He's a better man than you, is what I would say. Instead of talking, I pull into the cemetery near Denver, follow his instructions, and help him and his oxygen tank out of the car. I hold onto his elbow as we shuffle through the grass to the place he will soon, I pray, rest; next to the wife that probably had bruises on her skin as it decayed, evidence of a broken arm. I wonder if he thinks about that.

Apparently not, because he's calling her a bitch even now. I stand quietly staring at the plume to the north, funny how you can see things better at a distance, as he lets out a long stream of grievances, ending with her overcooked baked potatoes. Suddenly, he is crying. He takes a thin handkerchief out of his front pocket and wipes his nose, but the tears continue to slide down his face. This is the moment, I think. A moment of something genuine and true; perhaps some regret, perhaps some decent sensation. Atonement. But no. He is looking at his plot. He is feeling sorry for himself, angry that his time on earth will soon be over and that he will be here, quiet and quiet and quiet, full of rage and unable to unleash it, and that we will go on without him.

Yes, I want to say. Let's speak the truth. Your time has come. You will soon be rotting away. I will not give you a second thought. I will not feel numb, I will feel grateful and relieved for the sake of the planet and her people. My child will come as you depart. Though this event is relatively small in the big scope of things such as a burning planet, this changeover gives me great strength.

Reliable narration

TODAY I HAVE A FEVER. LIKELY IT'S THE TOOTH, A ROOT canal gone bad and the subsequent need to have number fourteen creaked out of my mouth. Perhaps it is a fever from life, a condition created from unreliable narration on a beautiful burning planet, and a viral infection affecting my cohort of peers. I'm a teacher with a fever. Ty, the Teacher. I did not become a taxidermist or a dentist, for better or worse.

§

Episodic writing, I tell my students, is worthy of your attention. Give it a try. You can get to the substance in small innocent-seeming tidbits, and several levels of truth can be revealed. Generally, there is some rooting to a "holding image" that serves as a connective device.

§

And sometimes life just feels episodic. For example, in this episode, I have been evacuated (mandatory, not volunteer) and so I have moved into TJ and Tam's house, mainly because their daughter Nastassja was a student of mine last year, and because it has an extra bedroom with its own bathroom, and because Gretel's house is crowded with the others, and because the truthiest truth: I accepted so as to spend more time with TJ.

§

When I teach my occasional course at the college as an adjunct, I always use the famous short story "Lust" by Susan Minot as an example (you can't teach that in high school, not if you don't want trouble). Look how the form *in*forms the content, I say. Look at how disjointed the narrator becomes from her own body as she has multiple meaningless sexual encounters! Her fragmentation is revealed in written fragments. My students love it because it's good and it's about sex.

§

I like sex, too, though I said *no* to your proposal, TJ, because you are in a relationship already, albeit a rotting one, perhaps because you are married to someone of the wrong gender. I don't know what's going on with you, or me, but I do know you're asleep down the hall, and I do know affairs are like a tooth infection, or like a fragment of a story, and I don't want any more of those.

§

Except, well, you know. Two souls connecting is rare. We all know it. We get lonely. We ask ourselves: What else is there, in life, other than love? So I *did* have a love affair with you in my mind, and it was lovely, because for a few moments, it was as if all the smoke was gone from wildfires here in Colorado, plastic gone from oceans far away, all rivers properly ran their courses, and all stories felt true.

§

I wasn't sure what to think about the YouTube my niece sent me to explain her love life. The YouTuber said: treat your love life like a TV series with lots of seasons and episodes, not like a long rom-com movie with one relationship that will last forever. I said to my niece: episodic stories are like that, best told in bits. But I wonder: isn't that how the planet got so bad, how we got so lonely? I said: responsibility. Commitment. That's another kind of love that takes *time*. She rolled her eyes, and I thought, poor Mama Earth, we treated her like a TV show.

§

Regarding teeth: when the dentist was bending over me to look in my mouth, I thought of his lower back, because dentists seem to have bad backs, just like teachers have tired eyes, like writers have achy wrists, like firefighters have calluses. As he looked at my teeth, I thought about his spine, and how in relieving some of my suffering, he was most likely causing some of his own. That made me sad. The virus makes me sad. I have started to grind my teeth at night.

§

So: I did well to avert our relationship. I heard what you said— with your vocal cords, your eyes, your body language—and I then reluctantly edited out that potential version of how this story could have gone. I am just a fuck-up human, lonely and lusty, and so I muttered, *true story, true story, true story, find the* true *story here.*

§

My tooth started *really* hurting last week, after a month of hurting vaguely—one example of my regular human humanness. Of course, if we had gone ahead with a tryst, we'd find something not to like about each other. I'd have food in my teeth, metaphorically speaking, and so would you. But also, know that I do not judge you. I know we're all just feeling crazy. We miss a healthy planet so we reach out like zombies to one another in order to prevent becoming zombies. You need to stay with your wife, Tam, a woman with a heart that aches. You need to stay with your daughter, Nastassja, a young woman who has a heart that aches. Yes, they have hearts too, and you need to stay. We all know that.

§

Betrayal of any kind now seems somehow related to Gaia's betrayal, and that is what I am trying to avoid. I want to reliably narrate a short story in honor of humanity and her future, in honor of complex hearts, in honor of our stunning inability to properly gauge the consequences of our actions. I want to write an apology letter for the many ways we have pulled Gaia's teeth. She feels hot when I press my bare feet to her forehead—do you feel it too? For restoration, we need re-story-ation.

§

Three days ago, I got the tooth pulled. And evacuated. Everyone is tired. Lice are going around. People are breaking up, people are getting together. But now I am sick. Maybe my fever is the result of anger at the innocent dentist, or teeth in general, or in the basic bad design we have, both emotionally and physically, or maybe it was that I'm angry with you. I tell my students: Write unreliable narrators: Dramatic tension! Except, of course, simultaneously do the opposite, and tell the story truer than true.

§

Maybe playing around with a heart is what a heart is for. When a heart comes snapping alive—well, that is something indeed! No one can foresee it, or stop it, or do anything except be mesmerized. That is what is happening now to us all, because of the virus.

§

Metaphor is the greatest act of writing. Look at *Gabriel García Márquez*'s story "One of These Days," I often say to my students. Consider the tooth that's being pulled (a *wisdom* tooth, no less). Teeth are great metaphors. Power, voice, voicelessness. Speak up! With metaphors!

§

Please imagine this is a story and it goes like this: today, here in Colorado, I have a fever, probably because we have free speech but not *frank* speech—a crazy drunk told me that last night. I miss the days when we had reliable narration and knew more or less whom to trust. Had long-term relationships. Although maybe those days never existed. But they could in the future, no? We could create whole and complete and inclusive stories.

Those days are coming.

They *could* come, at least.

New stories.

Reliable narrators.

Braver narrators. That's what this world needs.

Tam's renovation

MAYBE DEMOLITIONS ARE ACTUALLY RENOVATIONS, WHICH has me thinking that this world is being rebuilt big time— although, sure, right now it feels awfully torn apart. I say to myself, let's wait and see?

§

That's what I tell myself as the mandatory evacuation area creeps closer to my home and acre of land in the foothills. The nearby mountains are on fire, and so is most of the West. Demolished forests near and far land on my house in the form of ash, and as I turn on the sprinklers to prevent dry-grass fires and stare at the milky sky and red sun, I have to acknowledge that maybe this is what renovation feels like. Fires bring renewal, and these forests needed to burn. Their tinderbox status, like our society's, is real. This misery will lead to new growth. By that, I mean, wildflowers and baby aspen as well as the required changes to climate chaos.

§

The view is grim. The misery factor is high. The mood is bad. We hear that homes up the mountain have burned. Ours might be next. I'm at the dumbest foggiest place I've ever been as I watch my neighbors evacuate, and they are probably at the dumbest foggiest place *they* have been. This has become the big-gest fire in Colorado's history and evacuees stream down the canyon with their stock trailers loaded with horses and goats.

I have my own horses and goats to evacuate. In the mornings, the valley is socked in with smoke, and waking creates a despair in my chest I've never quite felt before—I thought I'd be more resilient, lifelong Coloradoan and all, and I sometimes feel close to having a true breakdown, whatever that means. I repeat my mantra: breakdown times are break*through* times! But still, my lungs and eyes and head all ache as I stare at the fog and feel the ash, and my cells, my very biology, urge me to flee. This does not feel like a breakthrough at all.

§

But I stay put as long as I can, in part because there's nowhere to go, and in part, because I've spent the entirety of the Great Isolation renovating two things—my psyche and my house. They are both long-haul repairs. Their renovations are important, demand focus, are a coming-of-age. Sure, ultimately both will be demolished—I will die, the house will crumble into the earth—but for now, I want to hang in there. I'm making such progress!

§

This home at the base of the foothills is a house I've bought twice and lost once. My husband and I bought it as a young couple; a decade later, he got it in the divorce; a few years later, I bought it back from him. The first time we moved in, when the kid was an infant, it was 1980s-weird but clean, as houses sold on the market tend to be. The second time I moved in, it was pretty trashed, inside and out. The ex left it as-is, that was part of the deal, which was fine but not easy. Pots and pans and expired food and broken skis and boxes of junk and dead mice were everywhere. No one had gone around with a baseball bat smashing stuff, to be sure, but it was wrecked, neverthe-less—via benign neglect, which feels similar to what destroyed the marriage, and that kind of slow decay is sad. Tiles falling off bathroom walls and wood rotting underneath, windows broken, dead skunks and packrats decaying in the floorboards. The acre of land, too, was hurting—chewed up by deer, dead and dangerous cottonwoods, fruit trees unpruned and looking like wild medusas.

I began the work of redesign. Walls were demolished, then rebuilt.

I met TJ. Nastassja liked him. We built a family.

Here we are.

§

My interior, my very *self*, well, that I've fixed up millions of micro-times and done a few big overhauls, too. I had a tough childhood and it took me a while to learn how to trust people, how to exist comfortably and kindly in the world. An abusive approach to religion led me to mindfulness trainings and a whole new belief system. Parenting changed me to the very core, as it does everyone. All this fixing-up has been real and tangible and solid. But there are more changes to come. I want to keep renovating myself.

§

Joy can be built. It stuns me, how different my life is with TJ and Nastassja, in this house. Even in a pandemic, even with our bifurcated country, even with this wildfire, I suppose there is basic happiness, basic contentedness, basic playfulness—at the *same time* as the sorrow. It's the same house and the same me, but this version of life is more artsy, colorful, experimental, and I'm not just talking about aesthetics or mood. Case in point: Paige, my druggie hippie friend, shared psilocybin tea, knowing I wanted mindful journeys for reconstructing my middle-aged brain. One day, exhausted from cleaning, I took some and went outside and lay in the grass and watched cottonwoods clapping at life, reminding me of the interconnectedness of it all, including viruses and humans, the pain of human suffering, and this quieter time for the planet, and hell yeah, I felt myself truly renovated.

§

Nastassja plans to get the coordinates of this place tattooed on her body. Fine by me. I feel for kids these days: jobs lost, internships gone, relationships impossible or stressed, and the fear of what is to come. To them, it feels like a demolition before it was time. They have the look of tired contractors trying to figure out the craziest project of their lives.

§

The house, my self, the family. Deconstruction, reconstruction. I believe people can change, but usually only when presented with a crisis that is real, immersive, tangible. Here is our time.

The wildfire rages. Small aspen will spring up.

The pandemic rages. We've learned flexibility and endurance.

Perhaps the house will burn, perhaps I'll die from a virus. We'll both crumple.

But in the meantime: the house is finally complete—framing, drywall, paint, floorboards, fixtures, windows, lighting. The yard is healthy—old trees trimmed, new trees planted, flower beds for birds and butterflies. My soul is fixed too, for real change like this reconfigures the brain. It's been exhausting. It might now burn. I need to start accepting that. But here's what I hope: the Great Stay has meant fixing these fixer-uppers. This is why I think the work of further reconstruction might now begin, and we can sweep the ash off the planks of the porches and find a cleaner way overall. Demolitions are the start of renovations. I say to myself: Hang in there, let's wait and see.

Naomi's chart of demise

I WOULD LIKE TO BEGIN, IF I MAY, WITH FOUR FACTS:

1. Mountain lions prefer deer but will eat llamas and children.
2. I have a daughter named Alexis who will someday have breasts and need a mammogram.
3. I have never gotten a manicure, but I do have pet chickens.
4. There is a wildfire bearing down upon my little town and in the day, we see ashen skies and swirls of smoke, and at night, we see the orange glow. We are literally the barrier. Everything west of us is now evacuated. There are no cars or trucks heading up the canyon anymore. There is not much to see.

Yesterday, I had my mammogram, which is never a joy but an acceptable part of the deal. The doc didn't like some glob on the black-and-white image, where tissues look like rivers and their tributaries, and so I was asked to stay longer for an ultrasound of my right armpit, which, unlike the mammogram, didn't hurt at all, but did make my heart ache with fear. The nurse said they'd call me when they could see what there was to be seen.

Fear. "Nothing is so much to be feared as fear itself," said Roosevelt, paraphrasing Thoreau, who probably paraphrased Francis Bacon: "Nothing is terrible except fear itself." Indeed. After the procedure, I decided to take the rest of the day off in order to combat fear. This is something I rarely do because I have a guilty conscience and am a mother.

Although I believe I know how to have fun (snowshoeing in silence is fun), it's possible that I am sort of a drag. Case in point regarding my puritanical past is that I haven't ever gotten a manicure. There are good reasons for this:

a) it would be stupid, given the way I use my hands in a rural kind of life;

b) all those chemicals and whatever-is-in-nail-polish-can't-be-good-for-the-planet; but

c) the real reason is because it hasn't occurred to me that it might be fun to take the half-hour to do so, because I have been too busy being busy.

To clarify my position: Manicures will never be my gig, I don't care how my nails look, but still, the mammogram made me want to do something for my body, and also I'd just had a fortieth birthday and every forty-year-old should have a manicure at least once, no? I thought I might lounge around, take a bath, read a magazine, and get a manicure, right in the middle of the day. Just to see what it was like. But then, the ultrasound made me late, and traffic in town was bad, the sky was gritty and gross, and when I got home, I was conscripted into making caramel popcorn, my signature meal. Then I got a call. From my mother in Wyoming. Did I want to come up? A mountain lion had just eaten one of her llamas on her ranch. Did I want to see?

So the next day, just to get outta town and a bit further from the smoke, Alexis and I drove an hour to my parents' ranch. And there, in the middle of a field, was a llama carefully covered in grass.

"Huh," I said. "We should probably get out of here."

"Weird," said Alexis.

"I want to see that lion," my mother announced. "My birthday is coming up. I want you to buy me one of those night-motion-detector camera thingies. If you love me, you'll do it."

The camera: so I did, at the nearby outdoor gear store. I have never had a breast ultrasound, and I have never purchased a motion detector camera.

Sees things in the dark, sees the forbidden, that's what those things do. So when I got home, I triple-checked the chicken house door. The wildfire is sending wildlife down our way. They'd prefer to be in the mountains, away from us, but since their mountains are burning, they come, like refugees, to us. I get it. But also we have seven chickens that follow us around when we step out of the house; they are mainly treated like pets, even by our dog. We all understand that we will lose them at some point: skunk, mink, mountain lion, bear, raccoon. All these carnivores have succeeded before, and they'll do it again. Things die. Usually while it's dark. But still. It's hard not to keep reaching out for love, despite the dangers.

Which is why I went upstairs and hugged my daughter, who was in bed, drawing all sorts of pictures of our neighbors, something she's doing a lot of lately, and as I hugged her, I begged the universe that her breasts would always be healthy. That this chemically smoke wouldn't lodge in her pure, sweet body.

This morning I got a picture of the mountain lion in an email from my mom. Beautiful. Huge. A male. Even in the black and white photo, I could see the blood of the llama on its mouth. Then a whole series of photos arrived: the lion sticking its head in the ribcage, the lion dragging the carcass out of view, the lion's butt, the lion's face. It occurs to me that I'd rather face a mountain lion than a cancerous cell any day.

After I showed the photos to my daughter, we drove into town and got a manicure. We picked regular old pink. Was that a good choice or not? Was spending $40 on nails really the best thing, with the un-homed man walking outside? Probably these chemicals *cause* breast cancer. I felt a little sick to my stomach. What was I *doing*? Sometimes our psyches operate in unusual ways. We can't take the view so we do something strange.

I came home and took a bath. In the middle of the day. I scented it with almond oil. I touched my breasts. I thought of cameras. I thought of the phone ringing with news. I thought of other women who were waiting, too. Or have waited. Or will wait. Of the ones who got good news, and the ones who got bad. I thought of women in the far past in all cultures, everywhere, who have felt a lump on their breast. Or who didn't, and got sick and died of something they didn't have an image of. I thought of my daughter. I thought of death. I noticed one pink nail had already chipped.

And now I stand at the window, watching, loving. I wonder what the lab report will look like. How it will be broken up and controlled in some sort of form with highlighted headers and fragmented information. I start calling this imaginary report The Chart of My Demise. I observe the fear. I wonder as to my psyche and what it needed, and why it chose a dumb manicure instead of some other thing.

The phone rings. The breast is fine. The wind outside gusts. I watch neighbors, such as TJ and Tam and their friend Ty, go for a walk in the sunset. I watch Nastassja trot up beside them on her horse. Then I see Mariana and Gretel and a dog wander past. Today, relief. No cancer. Yesterday, fear. To clarify my position, the camera sees things in the dark, sees things forbidden. Which is why, this morning I came home, and now I stand at the window, watching, loving. The sky becomes dark, so the glow of wildfire becomes visible, so I decide four things:

1. I commit to never getting another manicure and to always having chickens.
2. Because I cannot stop wildfire or wind, I will make some coffee for the firefighters who have no control over the forces either, but who are trying to keep us safe.
3. I will frame one of my daughter's images as that is the good kind of image and I shall always show her images like dead llamas so that she understands, on a cellular level, the circle of life.
4. I will think about creating a different chart, one that is less busy, perhaps to be called The Chart of Obstinate Joy.

Play, hands

I, LOU, HAVE LONG HAD THIS NOTION THAT I WANTED TO learn to play guitar before I died, which will be soon, a desire which stayed vigorously in the *vague someday* category because, let's be honest here folks, what I really wanted was to be magically playing guitar without the work of learning. I really did want to play, don't get me wrong, but maybe I was waiting to get hit on the head and concussed and then be magically able to play, like that guy I saw on TV. I never even picked up a guitar.

§

I think I am not alone in this desire to a) learn the guitar, b) someday, 3) without effort. We humans want all sorts of things to go like that.

§

Then COVID and wildfires came.

§

I am a middle-aged man with tough skin but the calluses now on my fingertips are even more firm. I trim my fingernails every three days. My rapid memorization of the chords, my attention to lyrics, my waking in the middle of the night to silently move my hands and practice chord progressions—this is strange. Strange, because I am a lazy person when it comes to things I find difficult, such as dealing with my neighbor or helping people, and musical instruments of all kinds. So this sudden focus and attention, well, I can't really account for it.

§

I can say, it is *not* because I have time on my hands, like those lucky people who bake bread.

§

Here's the truth: I think what happened was some deep wisdom inside that a) sensed big stress, b) was terrified for me, and c) gave me something new and hard to focus on in order to prevent lapsing into a despair coma, and d) simultaneously keeping a jelly jar out of my hand.

§

It's this last point that gives me pause. I think I am not alone in this go-to of drinking-while-stressed. Then trying to monitor it because, well, the dangers are obvious. This walking the line is as difficult as the G chord. But I am managing both.

§

When it grows cool, I pick up the guitar. I do it out of habit now, I don't even think about it. I also pour a glass of whiskey. Yeah, there is still a jelly jar of whiskey. There will always be a jelly jar. But there will be two jelly jars fewer because of the guitar.

§

I've had this thought before: The whole reason to limit drinking is to be able to drink in the future. To limit drinking means longevity of drinking. The effort is for future Lou, so he can have a glass of whiskey after dinner, forever. I might have another ten or twenty years or so I guess. So, I guess you could say it was an act of love?

§

My first songs are Prine, VanZandt, Cash, especially those that rely heavily on A and E since they are the easiest. I find D difficult and F impossible and my fourth finger seems to not connect with the others or my brain, which is something I didn't know about myself until I picked up a guitar.

§

I notice that my daydreams are about playing guitar around a campfire, and in my dreams, I sound rather fabulous, of course, because we are always the star of our own daydreams, but the larger point is that my brain is conjuring moments of *community*. Why? Because people daydream about what they are lacking. I wonder whatever happened with that truck that hit the deer. I wonder how all those people are doing. It stresses me out.

§

Addiction to the guitar is surely healthier than one to whiskey. These are sad days. I play sad songs. But also love songs, because love is an anecdote to sad. There are two forces that you can't mess with in life—mother nature and love. Mother nature is giving us a virus and wildfires and hurricanes, and love is a force we gotta sing into our lives. I'm past the idea that I'll find love—but I can still sing of love.

§

I'm worried about the winter, though, the cold, the dark, the alone, even if winter is what we all want, so as to put out this fire. But I know I might be tempted to pick up the jelly jar more than a few times, so my current brain tells my future brain this: trim your fingernails, pick a challenging song, one with a lot of Fs and Gs, and start playing. Get out and help people.

§

At the end of the evening, I stretch my hands out and consider them. My fingertips hurt and now my shoulder is hurting and my hands are tired. But I say: tomorrow, hands, play. You must keep keeping on. To learn things the hard way. Play, hands, play.

Our shifting fire

PETS, PASSPORTS, PHOTOS: THAT'S WHAT WE TOOK AT 3 A.M.
when the reverse 9-1-1 came, and soon after the volunteer search
and rescue guy pounded and yelled *Mikaela, get out, it's right there*,
and we could see the fire ourselves, the glowing rubble of fire
being swept at us with a huge broom of wind collecting debris
into our corner of the planet. We were moving fast and yet, for
a second, I stopped barefoot on the wooden floor to observe
the dissonance of my thoughts, turning from *but this is my home*
to *here the fire is.*

This wildfire, which had started so far away, was now crest-
ing Sleeping Bear Mountain again. Impossible. It was supposed
to be going in the other direction now. And yet, this glowing
ball.

How can the world shift so? The winds, the fire, my
thoughts, our life?

Then I moved, fast, to start the sprinkler system and my
son caught chickens and plonked them uncaged into the car.
They stood on car seats clucking and climbing over the golden
retriever and the cockatiels and boxes of diaries and photos. We
piled in and drove away, silent and scared, police lights flashing
in the dark, shifting from red to blue, red to blue.

§

We drove down the mountain, past the tents at Gretel's, then
north. My cousin's ranch is there, and by the time we arrived,

other evacuees were already congregating in the lighted kitchen. Their animals were being unloaded, too: a blind horse, donkeys, dogs. My cousin made coffee and my uncle stood at the window watching the plumes of smoke, confused by not only his Alzheimer's but by this sudden onslaught.

The sun rose; the sky lit. The winds continued to storm, huge plumes of smoke swirled, ash sifted onto our cars and into our lungs. Even from here, we could hear the sirens; the helicopters and tankers filled the air, taking water from the lake to fire. I felt seasick with confusion. Flee? Stick to home ground? I felt shifted apart, my bones and tendons and cells all slightly altered and too loosely strung together. Suddenly this was *our* tragedy, and the ever-present-newest-calamity on the news was ours, and I couldn't watch it with the semi-disinterested *ah, too bad for those people*, because there was no such protective thought to go to; no knowledge that it was them, and not me.

§

In the days following, surprising things shifted. Hummingbirds, for instance, appeared everywhere, driven down from the mountains. Deer, elk, bear, moose all appeared. Then, too, the fire shifted yet *again*, first away from our home, then toward. We studied perimeter maps from the kitchen table: the fire was within two miles, then one, then a half. Then we started counting in yards. Emotions shifted. These forests needed to burn, devastated as they are by the pine beetle. But a calmer fire would be better; a fire that could be controlled; a fire that wasn't gobbling up people's homes. Some were furious: the lack of prescribed burns, the lack of preparedness plan, the small initial response. And yet, simultaneously, there was awe and something way beyond gratitude: for the individual heroes, for the tanker pilots' skill, for wildland firefighters, for kids setting up lemonade stands with free lemonade and donations given to those now without homes. Joy for one person's luck, sorrow for another's loss. The After-Math Ranch burned, another place burned, and Kay is already dead. Ours, we don't know.

But the biggest shift seems to be in my body. It is painful—the real, tangible, excruciating anxiety that occurs when you can no longer self-guard, self-protect. There is no off-switch, no safer ground. I am stuck in my own body, facing the tragedy face-on. The guy at the post office, for example, standing in line with me to get our undeliverable mail, stared at me blankly and simply said that his home was gone, just gone, and that he had no insurance. And I thought: we humans can't truly embrace every horror, or else we'd be submerged in a nanosecond by the unspeakable suffering that this world offers. But at times like this, it does just that. Embrace the unspeakable suffering that is everyone, including starving children half a world away. Suddenly it was *all* in my heart, there in line at the post office. As much as I asked my mind to send me on a tangent, it simply would not. It could not, or it would not. It just left me hanging there, raw and open, gasping for breath.

§

When we were allowed to return home, we found a silent house coated with ash and dust. Black fine stuff on all the window-sills. Sleeping Bear Mountain has burned again, all the way to the river, but our side is fine. Nate and I are quiet, as if our talk would shatter the tentative fire line—the fire is still burning, after all. But we started to right ourselves again. Nate painted THANK YOU HEROES on plywood for the firefighters going by. We unpacked, we cleaned. We let our minds re-coat themselves with protective tangents. When the heat wave continued on the East Coast, I closed my eyes and let strangers' difficulties penetrate. Then I opened my eyes, and stopped. It is their catastrophe, not mine. How can I deal with both?

Perhaps it is the limitation of the heart that saves the heart, and it is the piercing which loosens, a little, what those limitations are. This fire has shifted my own protective coating, of that I am sure.

Installments of
the story of fire

ONCE UPON A TIME—AND THIS IS A TRUE STORY—I, GRETEL Rose Kahne, heard another true story about a wildfire in California started by migrants who had set a signal fire out of desperation. Here's how I remember it: they'd been left by the coyote, abandoned for weeks, were dying of thirst, were scared. Dying is scary. Their little signal fire turned into a wildfire, and I remember wincing, knowing the flames of xenophobia and anti-immigrant sentiment would be fanned too. Anyone would've built a fire, though. Yet: one more news story for Fox News to blow up, rather than discussing the dire conditions—and the U.S.'s role in them—that created that situation in the first place.

§

So, years later, I used that very event in a novel I was writing—I had the same thing happen fictionally, but in Colorado (because with fiction, you get to do things like that). As I wrote it, real fires were burning in Colorado, and I was evacuated, and there were fires in California and seemingly everywhere else in the West, too. A signal fire to us all, if ever there was one. That was about a decade ago. Then I wrote an unsuccessful grant application because I was curious about researching recovery.

§

When writing that novel, I asked some newly made friends to fact-check some details regarding secret routes of immigrant travel, because they knew. The novel was an attempt to articulate my feelings regarding social justice and the plight of *ilegales*, which no human is: let me repeat, no human is illegal. When the novel was published, I sent them a signed copy of the book in thanks, as is standard protocol, and because I was truly grateful for their assistance.

§

Then a thousand homes burned down near Boulder, one of them belonging to these friends.

§

There had been a terrible windstorm near Boulder. I live just an hour north, but our day had been calm and sweet. The unfairness of why one group of people gets to remain safe, while another group suffers, well, accepting that is one of the hardest parts of being alive—and my guess is that villagers in war-drug-lord-poverty-torn countries wonder about it pretty frequently, too. Now, it is my area that is burning again.

§

So, there was a fire in California. Then, a fire in Colorado. Then I wrote a novel. Then there was a fire in Boulder. And now my mountain is burning again. There are people in my yard. The community has kicked in in all sorts of ways—offers of animal care, free room-and-board, GoFundMe campaigns. Later, I got a boyfriend. And later, I found myself working on an essay about a water-drop I'd done with a humanitarian group in Arizona—that's where the highest number of humans die per year, often of thirst, and this last year was the most deadly on record. I had gone to the area as a journalist, more or less, to see how others help prevent what had happened to the migrants like the ones I'd read about in California, so many years ago.

§

The world is connected like this.

§

Repeats like this.

§

Dying migrants had asked for help by fire. I tried to help in a roundabout way with a novel about a fire. Friends had helped me with that novel, then their house burned in a fire. Now my house might burn in a fire, so I wrote another book about a fire. Because sometimes, you have to keep unpacking the same thing again and again and again.

§

This is how true stories go.

Norman's ten seconds
during the snow

YESTERDAY I WITNESSED A GREAT HAWK-AND-SPARROW drama with several plot twists and an unexpected ending. Let me say right here that I'm not certain what kind of hawk it was, maybe a Rough-Legged, perhaps an immature Red-Tailed hawk, I have no idea, because I only moved from General Bird Appreciation to Actually Trying Birdwatching since COVID, which was a humbling move, as all such moves are. It's hard to admit one has been basically lazy. Honing our observational skills really does matter to a life well lived, I believe that—but also, I am a regular human with regular human tendencies. I've been trying to up my game, though, and this has extended to bird appreciation.

So, what happened was this: I was recently cooking for the fire crew and then out on Search & Rescue and then it snowed overnight and the next morning I went to shovel snow off Gretel's deck and I happened to glance up at just the right second.

But first, the snow. It didn't really need to be shoveled, it could have just melted—the next day was forecast to be sunny and 60 in Colorado—but there I was for no good reason except I am human, and therefore I wanted to get out of the house, to do things like get fresh air and ward off backaches from sitting and blueness from winter and wildfires. So there I was, annoyed because it was still very cold and windy, not the sort of day you really enjoy being outside, but simultaneously needing to ward off dangers. It had been a tough year.

That's when I glanced up to see a flock of sparrows congregated on a patch of brown muddy dirt near a car, and right then, a hawk swooped down and picked up a sparrow, flew a few feet, and landed with it in its talons in the snow.

And there they sat for a few seconds.

I assumed the hawk would eat the sparrow, which felt like a good idea because hawks need to eat, too. But the sparrow kept cheeping, all the scattered sparrows kept cheeping, and I stood there waiting to see how this would play out, and then I said, "Dude!" because the hawk was sinking into the snow, flapping his wings. At the sound of my voice, he flew off. I had a moment of confusion: had he already eaten that little thing without me noticing?

Then a little head popped out of the snow. Such a tiny little head in a big expanse of white! We stared at each other, equally surprised, and then she flew off to a low branch.

I tromped through the snow so I could stand underneath her and looked up and said, "You okay up there?" and she took off, so the answer was, yes. Then I looked down at the patterns of the hawk's wingbeats and the little sparrow feathers scattered among the crystals.

That was only ten seconds of my day. But it was the most alive ten seconds of my day. Ten seconds in a day is all you really need, I suppose, to not only relieve backaches and heartaches but also to realize that instead of just knowing the vague difference between a hawk and a sparrow—a very vague distinction, to be sure—that you could take another step in the direction of being a better witness: Rough-legged Hawks have small feet, the better to perch on the smaller twigs toward the end of branches, which actually, somehow, really matters.

Look how safe it is
out there, Kay

WHEN KAY WAS ALIVE, SHE'D SHUFFLE DOWN SLEEPING BEAR Circle, and my dogs would go crazy, barking and advancing at her, snarling, backing up just enough to move out of the way of her advancing feet. As soon as I heard them, I'd jog outta the house to admonish them, embarrassed as I always was at these peace-loving dogs, who apparently would torment the mentally ill with their own insane behavior, which they reserved only for Kay, she who could least cope with yet another danger.

It would take several minutes of hisses and commands to get the dogs to retreat: Blackie-get-home, Badger-shut-the-hell-up, get now, get on home! Last time I saw her, I nudged them on their butts with my shoe to get them going and launched into apologies as I turned back around to face Kay. Her face was slick-wet with tears, which made me all the sorrier, and also con-fused, because I am unsure why she continued to brave these dogs. But she believed that walking one circle around our neigh-borhood and down onto my lands would protect her—from what, I don't know. UFOs or devils, I think. But it wasn't those entities who got her—it was the fire.

Bob the Younger, she'd say. Your dogs keep the world safe.

Which to anyone else would have seemed the opposite of true.

Mostly that day, I was in awe of her hair: the graying black matted and tangled with cockleburs, causing the strands to jut out this way and that, balls of matted hair to clump here and there. I did not ask about them, and she did not offer an explanation, but I knew from previous conversations what happened: she had been hiding in a ditch somewhere, crawling around to escape the UFOs that hover above her house and send down aliens through the chimney pipe to rape and hurt her.

I have heard something before about the use of aluminum foil around her body for protection, and the contraptions she has placed in her house to trick devils, stories of paranoia and pleading conveyed in repeated sentences that stop and start and circle around. The sort of stories that would be creative and amusing, I guess, except for the terror in her darting eyes.

She didn't call me Bob as everyone else does. She called me Bob the Younger since she remembered Bob the Elder, my father.

She mumbled things like, Bob the Younger is a safe man. His dogs are safe.

I invited her in that last time, right before the first voluntary evacuation, before we knew how bad it would get on that one windy night, and I asked if she wanted coffee or tea, but she refused. Words tried to form themselves in her mind. Her mouth opened and closed, her eyes shut in a moment of concentration, and a wave of confusion crossed her face.

I wanted to help her, but all I could do was watch her struggle. If I had been a better person, I would have stood behind her and cut out the burrs from her hair, offering to wash it afterward in the sink, and while I was at it, wash her filthy clothes too. We had time. Bob the Elder would have done that. Bob the Elder would have somehow convinced her to get in his truck before the evacuation. Bob the Elder wouldn't have scared her off. Bob the Elder would have saved her.

Instead, I sat calmly at first, unsure and awkward, and hating myself for it. *Activity manifests the essence*, I was told as a child. A hundred, a thousand times. Who you are is what you *do*, and yes, surely some action or kindness is better than nothing; better to rush forward and fail than to sit about weighing choices.

And so then I did move, even reached out and touch her trembling hand, and I told her, *We really must go. There's an evacuation. It might burn here. Come with me.*

She jerked her hand back and glared at me. Once her words came, there was no stopping them. The fire is the work of the devil! Nine-one-one. Bob the Younger was the devil! Did I know, did I know, did I know that the date, nine-eleven, is the same as the phone call for help, and did I see that big explosion on TV, those buildings, and did I know that was the work of Satan, too? Didn't I know that Obama had come to spread the Good Word but that Evil had found the way? Where was the rain? Why has God sent wind and not rain? Why didn't I talk to God? Even God would listen to his Brother, Satan.

I tried to stay calm. I was stressed. I offered again to take her off the mountain. I insisted. She refused and cursed me. So I decided to just call the sheriff and told her that when I returned, I'd bring cat food and some new books of poetry, and bird seed for her feeders. I told her that although the air was filled with smoke, somehow it was still a beautiful day, and it seems like all the bad in the world was very far away, didn't it? During the moments I said this, I winced at my own failure to be the sort of person I wish I was.

And now, even as I stand staring at her burned house, her bones taken away by the coroner, I remember my last words to her: *Look,* I'd said, nodding at Sleeping Bear Mountain with its green trees, *it'll be okay, look how safe it is out there, Kay.*

Now I'm home, and it's snowing, and I'm watching the snow build in the crevices of the mountainside right in front of me, and I console myself with those same words.

Fire Ice

ONE THING I'D LIKE TO GET CLEAR ONCE AND FOR ALL: YES, that orange stuff, AKA Fire Ice, that you see flying from airplanes, is toxic. Looks like reddish carrot juice misting from the skies. Feels like slime. And yeah, they sometimes use it for show: high-profile fires with media present. And it's likely used in cases where it's going to have very little effect, but, well, fire managers ask for it and they're going to use it because it looks like they're trying to do something, which they *are*. Don't get me wrong— this is a complicated subject—I'm not saying air assets do not play a critical role. They do. Air assets themselves are not for show, but I want to take a look at Fire Ice.

The Forest Service, etc. will tell you it's not toxic. "Non-toxic, non-corrosive, and no impacts on terrestrial or aquatic wildlife" is what's up on the USFS webpage. It depends on what you mean, I suppose, by "toxic." Certainly, they've made it less toxic now. At least it doesn't have stuff that turns to cyanide, basically. But even the current stuff is toxic to aquatic creatures. Most retardants are ammonia-based, so aquatic life is sensitive to that—acutely, right after delivery. We have mitigations—they are not supposed to deliver it near water, for example, that's a national policy—not within 300 feet of a waterway. But let's also agree that the VLATs—Very Large Air Tankers—cannot be that specific.

Also, look at our past history of saying things were safe.

Also, look at the studies of invasive species and weeds coming in after usage.

Also, let's look at all those fish that died in California in 2009.

Also, the cost of retardant drops is staggering.

But also, maybe most importantly: look at all the places it's been dropped and it appeared to do nothing. Except make people feel that something was being done. Fifteen, twenty million gallons of this stuff dropped last year. Greenwashing with orange, is what I call it.

Yes, it does retard fire, gives firefighters time to build lines, and it's true that you can use aircraft to change where the fire is, such as knocking it out of the canopy and putting out the surface fire with ground-based forces. That's a fact. I'm trying to say that the situation is nuanced. For example, the effectiveness of it varies depending on fuel—it generally works better in grasslands, but not so much in the forested canopy. And you certainly don't just drop it and it puts the fire out like some people think. You need people there on the ground to take the next step.

The only thing in favor of it is, yeah, if it keeps more toxic stuff from burning and being released into the air, then it's the lesser of two evils. But let's just keep our story honest. Our facts straight.

Let's agree: wildland firefighters are going to ask for whatever they can get, for good reason: a VLAT, helicopters, crews. And air assets are expensive and not in ready supply and I understand that you fight fires based on a plan with strategic objectives and available resources. Like nearly every human in every situation, they're going to ask for all the options until someone says no. Including the Orange Stuff. Unless someone smart says, hold up. Let's think about this. How useful is it here? What are the dangers? Indeed: I wonder, what is each person's equivalent of orange stuff? What do we do for show? Toxic though it may be?

Books found at Kay's house

THE FIREFIGHTER HAD NEVER HEARD ANY OF THESE NAMES, though the books looked glossy and recent, which meant such people existed out there somewhere, scribbling away, at this very moment. These were not dead authors, but living authors, and unburned authors, and much-loved authors, their books being marked-up and sticky-noted and dog-eared.

The whole room was black and dripping. But this one bookcase stood in the middle of the room and thus presumably was the one that held the most sacred books. The titles she was scanning were from the middle section of the row of books, in the middle bookcase, on the middle shelf, which somehow had escaped both fire and the worst of the water. She ran her finger across their spines:

Conflict Resolution for Holy Beings by Joy Harjo
The Hurting Kind by Ada Limòn
Black Nature: Four Centuries of African American Nature Poetry,
    ed. by Camille Dungy
Uplake by Ana Maria Spagna
Plainsong by Kent Haruf
Rise, Do Not Be Afraid by Aaron Abeyta
Not for Luck by Derrick Sheffield
Native Voices: Indigenous American Poetry, Craft, and Conversation
    ed. by CMarie Fuhrman and Dean Radar
Dwellings by Linda Hogan

The Home Place by J. Drew Lanham
Braiding Sweetgrass by Robin Wall Kimmerer

She stepped back and surveyed the burned shelves and burned books and burned walls. Many books had fallen to the floor and were soggy and foamed at her feet, including what looked like a bunch of diaries. It was time to go. The firefighter reached into the case and retrieved one slim book from this middle section, chosen for its dusk blue color. The only book back at her own home was *How to Deer-Proof Your Yard*, which had proved to be wildly unsuccessful, and suddenly she was struck with how empty her life was as evidenced by the lack of books. She wanted this book instead. She wanted all these books. She wanted to understand poetry and what it offered and vowed that now she would point her ship in that direction.

Salvage operations would be here to gather Kay's things for her daughter, so the firefighter sighed heavily and slipped the book back. *Integrity, courage, honor, selflessness, and servitude, never to be compromised.* She repeated it in her mind for strength, because she *knew* this blue book of poetry would prove more useful in her life than her deer-proofing book, she *knew* this book was something Kay would want her to have. But no. She'd go to the local bookstore. Which was, after all, called Old Firehouse, built in an old firehouse, and she would buy all the blue books she wanted.

Still, though, she pretended. She held an imaginary book to her turnout coat as she walked out of the smoldering house, shoulders bent with exhaustion and the weight of this fire season and her world still devoid of poetry.

Kay's notebook

I JUST DON'T KNOW WHAT CODE THERE IS IN THIS WORLD, BUT I believe it's our duty to figure out codes, and I believe in coding, which is what I once did.

Love will come as many times as you want it, as long as you do the work to find it, and I love the cats, the moose, the raven, the bear, the mountain mahogany, the chipmunk. But each time love comes and you give of yourself, it will deplete you as well as simultaneously fill you up. It's a matter of dehydration and saturation. Resisting and persisting.

So the question really is: do I love the world? And what will love *do* to me? I am starting to work it out.

$$(1) \; Happiness = f(Good \; Health, Love, No \; Virus, Safe \; Future)$$

And happiness is equal to the sum $\sum$ of all its parts:

$$(2) \; Happiness = \sum_{i=1}^{3} \; l_i \; where \; i = (Good \; Health, Love, No \; Virus, Safe \; Future)$$

But if things get coded badly, then:

$$(3) \; Depression = \sum_{j=1}^{2} \; k_j \; where \; j = (Hope \; Gone, Sleepy)$$

So when the view of my expected future life, $E[life]$, is constant tired, _pain_:

(4) $E[life] = \underline{pain} = OK$ to Run. Run where? Run away from this mountain?

But if it's *OK to Die*:

(5) $E[life] =$ *need to work this out so I can stay*

§

I am so thirsty, the emotionally dehydrated kind of thirsty. On this bit of land I have, there are streams and they run through fields like capillaries in the brain and body. Simple formulas are easy to solve and are the purest. The clichés of the Western night sky are true, and I suppose clichés are clichés for a reason, and as the night deep-darkens I can in fact see the Milky Way and all the closer crazy-bright stars as the world sleeps. The smoke is blowing south. People who do not live up here do not know how bright the sky is.

I have to open the door to get to know the planet better. I have to say, Planet, I have these fears. I'm a smart woman and I've done my research. For example, did you know that a plethora of theories have arisen to explain schizophrenia? Such as:

- miswiring of the brain during development
- an inherited disorder exacerbated by stress and hormonal changes
- autoimmune damage
- depletion of certain fatty acids in cell membranes
- a transmissible viral infection

That last one is the big one. And that virus comes from cats. Or cat feces, to be specific.

Viruses have been attacking us all along. And
$E = $ expectation

My $E[life]$ is changing:

Current life = set A, made up of little a's

a_1 = I am in Colorado.
a_2 = The virus is far away. I am SAFE HERE. Bob's dogs
     protect me.
a_3 = The mountain is good. This river is good.
a_4 = The brain's weirdness can be hidden. I can just STAY
     QUIET.
a_5 = Do not let the neighbors know.
a_6 = Concentrate on the night sky and sleep during the day.
a_7 = My daughter names things. Agoraphobia. Schizo-affective
     disorder.

(6) $E[life] = \sum_{i=1}^{7} a_i$ = I will keep walking forward. I will learn
about the planet and space and skies and Colorado.

E is what you expect to happen from random unknowns. I'll tell
Mother Earth the truth, that she is a random singular unknown.

There are many ways of not feeling well, of feeling sick, and
I sometimes think God had a sidekick to come up with ways
to make humans uncomfortable. Cramps. Broken bones. Nerve
pain. Brain pain. Brain confusion. This sidekick of God has the
sobriquet of "Brainstormer of Misery," and I'd like to give him
a talking to someday.

What do most of us want? We want someone to see the
hurt done to us in this world, and we want someone to care. And
if we find someone who *does* care, well, then. That's something.

I do remember the list and it's important that I remember lists right now and my list was called "Random Interesting
Information About Schizophrenia."

- 2.7 million Americans have schizophrenia.

- One-in-five will recover.
- Schizophrenia has been linked to mothers having rubella during pregnancy.
- It's been linked to older fathers, but not older mothers.
- Siblings who are born around the same time have a much higher chance of getting it than siblings born many years apart. This supports the idea that it is set off by a virus…viruses shared more often between siblings of the same age group.
- The states with the highest number of ticks also have the highest rates of schizophrenia. As in, VIRUS.
- People with schizophrenia have a very low rate of rheumatoid arthritis, in fact, they are virtually immune from the disease. There's a hypothesis that arthritis and schiz are the flip sides of the same gene, whose expression is sparked by a virus, and a tendency toward schizophrenia is in fact a genetic "trade-off" for a resistance to arthritis, and vice versa.
- Persons with schizophrenia have more dopamine. When you fall in love, you have a lot of dopamine.

NOTICE the prevalence of VIRUS.

Virus, virus, virus. Second of all, my mother was older, yes. Third of all, we had cats. And finally, please notice the word *recover.*

I can say without a doubt that I am happier and safer than I have ever been. I'm not alone here. The code is almost cracked.

Piñyon

THE PIÑYON TREE WAS TIRED ALREADY, THOUGH YOUNG. Piñyons were *born* tired. She wasn't sure why this was, but she sometimes asked the sky about it. "These things happen," the sky said on this particular occasion. "I dunno. I feel quite young most days, younger than you felt even when you were an inch tall and all new and soft green, even when you were three-feet-tall and planted here by Kay's daughter to attract the birds. Even *then*, you felt old. All you piñyons just look so tired. Even you youngsters."

"Well, you look tired today, Sky," the piñyon said.

"Yes, siree-bob," Sky mumbled sadly. "Today I am. Today I contain the ashes of poetry and all their wisdom makes me feel quite aged. Quite tired with the burden of knowledge and heartache."

"You'll read me one, then?"

Sky hesitated. "I guess so. Although I get weary of these humans assuming they are the only ones who tell stories worth hearing. The whale's songs, for instance. Now *those* are some stories I wish I could share with you. But okay, okay. We'll patiently listen to them. I see a wisp of flying paper right here. Okay. Here we go. Let's read some words that someone so carefully put together and see what these humans have to say."

All this witnessing

SHE WAS SO TIRED. GRIT AND BROKEN BITS OF ASPHALT pressing at her knees. Curled like an armadillo, or perhaps a sleeping bear. That's what she looked like from afar, but Gretel wouldn't have known it, because what she knew was exhaustion and grief, having finally broken on a simple walk to her neighbor's house. She knew the difficulty of breathing and sobbing at the same time. She knew the smell of her skin and gravel, since her face was pressed into elbow crooks, forearms wrapped around head, palms covering ears, and her nose right above warm rocks and grasses that bordered the road. As if bombs were exploding, as if she were doing a duck-and-cover, as if she was broken, as if she was done.

It was the stinging pain of flesh rubbed raw on knees that finally gave her reason to push herself to the side, sit up. From here, she could see Alexis and Naomi's house. Which is where she'd been walking. To simply tell them that Sierra, the fisheries biologist, had heard from someone that the upcoming twelve hours would be decisive about whether the fire would wrap back around and head toward them, and that, once again, they should be ready to go, that the chances of the town burning were real again, and given the wind, well...*Prepare thyself.* That's what she had said, that's what Gretel's inner voice said, that's what the world was saying. *Prepare thyself.*

So she looked at Naomi's house and beyond that, TJ and Tam's house, and beyond that, out of sight, the dairy. And above her, also out of sight because of the first foothill, the homes of all the others. A moment of pure being. Dazed and yet suddenly overwhelmed with an enormous intake of sensation. As if the tears had wiped her soul clean and she could now re-hear and re-see everything. The grasses and pavement smelled like heat that had continued too late into the year, smelled like propane, smelled like dead animals. A tiny noise in the grass and her eyes found a wasp-like creature and it took her brain a moment to place it, a Tarantula Hawk, dipping itself into its burrow in the ground. And then, amazingly—what were the chances?—a scurry nearby. An enormous spider. Moving toward her. She squinted. A tarantula? No, a Carolina Wolf Spider. It moved to the right and her eye followed its path and she saw an enormous fat caterpillar with one eye, yes, only one eye. A dead doe had once been here. Had been replaced by all this.

She felt high. As if the details of the world were being pulled into her eyes and nose and ears by some magical force, but no, she was not high, this was just Planet Earth.

She tried for the 6-4-7 breathing. Needed to calm. Or was it 7-6? Big breath in. Slow release. Touched her knees, the right one scraped enough to be bleeding. Picked out small pebbles from the mush. She did not have the strength to stand. She wiped at her wet face with her forearm because now the wet from tears was beginning to tickle.

A gawky teenage blue jay squawked at her from a tree and flew to her blue birdbath. There, it shared drinking with a gawky teenage robin, the two of them bobbing up and down on opposite ends of the blue bowl. They seemed to drink forever. So greedy for water. And suddenly she was thinking of all the water below her, in deep underground waterways that forced molecules through layers of stone. How far down? What did it sound like? What was the earth like deep down there? Through how many millions of nematodes and bacteria and worms and other living things? Then she looked up. If only it would snow again. Eventually, it had to; the patterns of mother nature were reliable that way. But for now, the sky was still pulsing blue, and not only that, there had been no clouds for so long that the sky itself seemed to screech, just as the blue jay had, wanting its bowl of water.

She registered two dogs barking in the distance and was struck by how different they were, one dog barking anxiously and incessantly and in need of a better owner, the other dog barking in a happy-dog way at a deer or some passerby. As she listened, her eyes found an anomaly in the ditch barrow, a pile of bear scat with lots of plum seeds. The wind was picking up and her hair lifted and brushed her face. God, how strange. All this witnessing. All this making sense.

She leaned forward and kissed her knee, as if it were some child separate from her. Then sat back, considered the whole valley. Her community. The rise of the foothill covered with mountain mahogany and their corkscrew seeds catching the sun. The yellow rabbit brush. And so, so many yellow grasses, grasses that were old and tired and leaning into winter. The enormous cottonwoods along the ditch bank, yellow and half-bare now. The season was on the cusp of changing.

She considered all that humans had done to this place before her: houses, gravel, asphalt, yellow lines, mailboxes, and yeah, they had torn up what once was scrubby meadowland, and she wished she could see it a thousand years ago. And a thousand years from now. And what would it mean? To have it destroyed? Others towns had just disappeared after fire, after all. Just gone, poof: California, Alaska, Oregon. And this one? This sweet little enclave? Just gone tonight? Tomorrow? The next day?

Just gone. She let out jagged air. Wondered if she had the strength to rise. Wondered at herself, as if from a distance. How she'd just broken down like that. How she'd been walking and simply had an image fly into her mind: of all these houses blackened and smoking and COVID and politics and wildfire and Planet Earth black and burned and stream of toxic smoke lifting into the air. And she'd just doubled over, had no choice but to fall to her knees, to release the sobs that had been stored up inside for so long, had to cover her head for protection. No more, no more, she could take no more.

Now her face was dry from tears and felt tight. Her eyes stung and would sting the rest of the day. A headache would press against her skull. She was thirsty. That's why she hated crying, it just wiped her out, wiped her so completely clean. She used her forearm to catch some snot, but discovered a streak of blood. Then, as she somehow suspected it would, she saw the old red truck in the distance, coming down the hill toward her.

In which Alexis tells the story
of her lemonade stand

HOLY-MOLY, MY BRAIN IS SUPER-CHARGED WITH THE ELEC-
tricity of learning so much stuff:

Pyroaerobiology is a field of study just invented and it's about
living organisms thrust up into the air during fires. Like fungi,
which is, like, you know, mushrooms, and fungal spores are *hurled*
up into the air in smoke and 350 quadrillion microbes are emit-
ted for every three acres burning in high-intensity fires, and like
80 percent of them are still living and that's crazy if you ask me.

There are four kinds of smokejumper parachute styles: the
main, which is the usual one that blooms out when the jumper
leaves the plane. The *reserve* which is for emergencies, and it's on
the jumper's chest. The *round FS-14* is a traditional parachute
and the *square Ram-Air* is used especially in lots of wind. I also
found a beat-up, snowed-on purple notebook in the ditch next
to the street and it says "Incident Response Pocket Guide" and
wowza the type is so tiny it short-circuits my brain with electricity but also I'm going to read it all and learn it all and become a
firefighter. As well as a painter. A painting firefighter. It's been
decided.

I learned that Gretel is in love with Norman (yay) and Paige
kissed Sherm (ick) and the teenagers broke up (sad). So: love
starts and then it stops. I'll remember that. I didn't know Sherm

before this fire and I think he's scary-looking although my mom says "he's a little rough around the edges, but edges usually smooth over with time," and he says he learned that the Colorado State Patrol can issue a carcass tag to legally possess a road-killed animal, so I guess I now know that, too.

Korine will have a baby. Her grandfather will die. So, life comes and then goes. I'll remember that too.

I learned some new words, like *la paja* is straw in Spanish and *my-kuh* is Ute for hello.

A whole gaggle of tired-looking, sooty firefighters came by in their really smelly outfits and drank everything I had and it made me want to cry how grateful I was and also because they all looked to be such good friends and I hope to have a group of friends like that someday. I also learned that there are kinda two groups of firefighters, the "careers" versus the "volunteers" and in this fire, they're getting along because they all need each other, and promise to do more of that because what they have in common is that they all care.

I learned that more houses burned up the mountain. I met a woman named Ammalie who was traveling across the country and sleeping in her car and I met a woman named Azura who told me about digging up a dead guy's grave (adults are so weird!) and I met a married couple who are smokejumpers (who have to be the coolest people ever). I met a woman named Autumn whose clothes were covered in spray paint. Nastassja told me I could be in her play and also that she'd teach me to ride horses. Ty the Teacher told me I'd probably love fifth-grade Colorado history and that we were sadly making it right now.

I learned this:

Backfire: is when crews set fire on purpose to get rid of fuel, like, an offensive strategy on a big scale.

Burnout: is routine firing to clean and improve the line of fuel, like, when a line is built, and a defensive strategy.

Let-burn: is an area where firefighters will let the fire burn.

Burnover: is when a wildfire is bad and it's an emergency situation and most of the time it means fire shelters were deployed and I don't even want to think about that.

Please don't think I'm crazy, but it's not only the people who talk. The trees talk, too, and they are really smart. And the birds. I even thought I heard the mountains talk and I swear they said: *Good mernin! Are you lollygagging around? Criminy! Good for you! Tell those frackers to knock that sh$t off right meow. Mmkay? For the sake of you, good kid!*

I learned that Ty the Teacher likes pink lemonade more than yellow. But Paige likes yellow because she says it looks more natural. TJ and Tam like hot cocoa, and Gretel likes coffee. It's a multi-purpose lemonade stand and Ty says that's called a "hybrid form."

I learned that These Are Hard Times. COVID made it worse. No one knew if we should take in other people, or if we might be killing people if we did. And the planet isn't so healthy. And that adults kinda knew they were coming, these hard times, but that they didn't "get it together in a big way," as Gretel says, and for that she is sorry. Maybe they are all sorry. I am the youngest person around, so they all look at me with those eyes. Those eyes that say, ut-oh, we made a mistake. But they buy lemonade to make up for it. Even though it's starting to snow out, and I'm cold, I hand out the cups and they take them because they don't know what else to do.

Obituary for a {wild} fire
as told by Blue Sky, Colo

You fuckers were borne of Smokey Bear and
Mother Nature, nurtured in the cradle of
climate chaos, and what well-nourished, big
beasties you grew to be! We had the opport-
nity to intimately know the two healthiest
of you—the first and second largest wildfires
in Colorado history, records made right in
front of our eyes—so we can attest to your
hale and hearty condition. Your life was
outrageously flamboyant! And your legacy will
be stupendous, and the next year will prove
it so, in our lungs and on our lands.

It's your prolific overpopulation that
sets you apart—an incredible 1,016 wildfires
have burned just in Colorado this year. And
your extended family—wow!—according to the
National Interagency Fire Center, 46,000 of
you were burning nationwide, eating up eight
million acres in 2020, which is two million more acres than the ten-year average.
Indeed, while we are most acquainted with
the Colorado branch of the family, my condo-
lences extend far beyond—California, Washington, Oregon, Arizona, Montana, and Idaho
are all still reeling from your fecundity.
Birth control is something we wish we'd all
considered.

As in, prescribed burns.
As in, less dependent upon fossil fuels.
As in, seeking Indigenous wisdom.

As in, intergenerational equity, and respect for the future. Caring more about being excellent ancestors rather than dutiful descendants.

Willing and accepting of change.

These are the things we should have done—and perhaps still have time for.

Your impact will be remembered. Like the lakes of fire in Revelation or Dante, your flames have caused a lot of hellfire, covering our houses and lungs in ash, evacuating friends, burning homes, and sending cortisol levels sky-high, as high as your billows of smoke. You created a strange contradiction of sounds, such as the constant drone of helicopters, paired with the quiet presence of stressed mountain animals seeking shelter. An elk in our yards. A limping bear with a burned paw up the mountain.

You had unique small effects as well, such as the increased use of spray paint—either for phone numbers on horses or plywood signs for firefighters. Who imagined you would spawn such creativity?

Finally, let us speak to your future legacy. It is secure. Now that we're allowed in the mountains, we can still smell the smoke, and we have bent down and picked up handfuls of burned pine needles and remembered our favorite spots, the places we picnicked or read books or skied or made love. Our forests are changed. Also, since you were a high-consumption fire, our soils are hardened and will not regrow naturally. Everything from water quality issues to future flooding, here we come! So, don't worry—you will not be forgotten.

So, your population, your size, your impact, your legacy—in all these ways, you have been oh-so-successful.

We dedicate this obituary to one in particular, for we have a special relationship with you, Cameron Peak Fire, you who
tormented us the most, living for one-hun-
dred and thirty days—put out only by December snow—an extraordinarily long life for
a creature like you. You did a great deal
of damage in that span, giving us hacking
coughs, bloody noses, headaches for months,
cancers, and lungs forever scarred.

A year is a long time to not feel well,
though some of us managed by breathing our
sorrow into words, writing fiction and nonfiction and poetry about you. As Amitav Ghosh
writes in *The Great Derangement*, "Unusual
events being necessarily limited in number,
it is but natural that these should be excavated over and over in the hope of discovering a yet undiscovered vein." Which is why
we need so many stories.

We keep hoping to discover the vein of
truth of how to live well now.

Memorial services have been held everywhere. We have raised glasses of whiskey
and herbal tea to your demise. Tree plant-
ings will now occur. Mulch will be dropped
by helicopter. Neighbors will help neighbors rebuild homes, regardless of their warring yard signage. Some neighbors have even
fallen in love. Some have had great sex. Some
became friends. Some have adopted a dog. Some
decided to move away. Some will stay until
their last breath. Some will watch the moose
and bear and ravens with a bit more gratitude. A better government that creates and
sustains various forms of health—for that
is why we have government—could be borne.

Ceremonies of acceptance shall now com-
mence. You are a sign of a sorrowful truth of
the rest of our lives, and, as with a little

virus, we must wrap our brains around new realities, of a changed world, of fires that will burn longer and brighter and faster. We must make peace with Hades spewing out bolts from below. We must then do what we can to decrease your power.

Onward we go. We ask only for peaceful reprieves so that we can have a proper burial and eulogize you, starting with telling a few of our stories.

Sleeping Bear speaks to Nova

NEVER A GOOD SLEEPER BUT THIS WAS THE FIRST TIME *SMELL* was the reason. Scent of wildfire mashed into Nova's nose, her dreams, her lungs, her brain. Acrid, chemical, full of things recently alive, full of spores, full of ash, full of dead animals, full of loss. It was *bad* and it was *inescapable*. The smell kept her on the move during her first night home: first in bed, then on couch, then back in bed, thrashing, twitching, finding itches.

It had been a month dead, that fire, and Nova had missed the entire chaotic mess by taking her first trip overseas. Clearly, though, she would not be absent for the consequences—she'd been told the smell would last a year or more. Surely it wouldn't be this *strong*? Head still on pillow, she opened her stinging eyes to Sleeping Bear Mountain, now lit with the first dull light of morning sun. She'd not been able to see when she'd finally arrived home last night, but now, oh now, there was the view that signaled *home*, the same view she'd had for four decades. But it was not the same at all.

"Ah, Bear, oh, Bear oh Bear," she murmured. "Oh, poor Bear. What did someone's campfire do to you?"

§

You're back again. Sleeping Bear's voice was not a low and rumbly voice—how cliché that would be!—but rather a sprightly whisper which only some creatures could hear and the rest mistook as breeze or mysterious mountain background noise. *Check out the aspen along the riverbed. Wooeee. Spared. You missed those golden leaves lit with the buttery morning light. Bonkers, right? Mmmm-mmmm. I see your eyes resting there on their bare branches, white against the blue of morning. This stand made it, they sang and sang their way to safety. I feel the sun lighting me up. Mmmm again, never fails to delight me. Anyhootles, welcome back. Missed you, I suppose.*

§

Sleeping Bear Mountain was burned, completely changed, but not burned as Nova had expected. Not at all. Her eyes felt confused. The pine trees were not *disappeared*, they were not fallen *down*. No. Most stood valiantly, red-brown and burnt and dead. Other pockets consisted of gray trunks with all the needles gone, so they looked like telephone poles, or blackened huge spears plunked down by a giant. And oddly, there were a few pockets of green—small areas of refugia—and she could figure out no rhyme or reason to their survival, perhaps shifting winds, perhaps surrounded by just enough granite.

"Missed you, Bear," she whispered to the mountain, which had now fully separated itself from night and stood stately and defined in the pale blue of morning sky.

She could have returned home sooner. The mandatory evacuation had been lifted weeks ago, though the electricity was not yet back on. But she'd been in Italy. In a moment of insanity—the wildfire certainly engendered those—she'd bought a ticket to Rome and caught a bus to Urbino and walked the cobbled streets of the walled city. Sometimes went to the beach and stared at ocean. Once went to San Merino, which was its own country inside of Italy, which she hadn't known about and thought was crazy. But the travel made sense. After all, her Fire Go-Bag had her passport and medicines and clothes, so when she evacuated, she figured she might as well keep going rather than stay in a smoke-filled and stress-filled America. She didn't even email her neighbors and friends. She just disappeared, poof, like a puff of smoke, so that she could enter into an entirely different story. She'd had interesting coffees and an interesting affair with a man and silently fallen in love with a woman. She was surprised by the small things of travel, like gelato being a different and better creation altogether. Or, most surprising of all, the air being muggy, moisture not something she'd remembered. She'd used up every last cent of retirement and now, at age sixty-six, she'd have to…well, go back to work, or go to the food bank, or who knew. She'd figure that out tomorrow when the jet lag cleared. One story at a time, she figured.

§

Well, you *look happy*, the mountain chirped. *Halle-damn-looya. I'm doing pretty good, too, actually. What an adventure! It's been a long time since I burned. Hundreds of years. Thousands, maybe. I lose track of time. Though I remember the wowzer transitions. When I was shallow ocean and beach. Uplift. Tectonic plates crashing. I've felt too dry for too long. I kinda needed to burn, though maybe not this way, it did feel like a kablamo firestorm. Too hot, too fast, too out of control. Not easy, even for me. Not easy for creatures in my care. But here we are.*

§

Head on pillow, Nova's eyes sought out some pattern on the old Sleeping Bear. Before the fire, her eyes had understood the mountain—green expanses of lodgepole and ponderosa with some fir and spruce and aspen thrown in and some willows down low. Now, she saw four categories: 1) the orange needles on partially burned pines, 2) the black sticks of more-burned pines, 3) small areas of surviving green, and 4) the granite rock faces and tumbles. Orange, black, green, gray. The colors were new, but so was the entire layout. Since trees no longer obstructed her view, there was far more rock, and since bits of hard snow were falling and sticking in the crevices, the drainages within that granite were visible. One little crevice led to another. Funny, what you could see when the outer layer of something was taken off. This was the earth's skin and resembled the older woman she was becoming herself—hair thinning, crevices of face, fractals of a different pattern.

She reached for her backscratcher, little fingers on a stick, so she could scratch the one itch on her left shoulder she could never reach herself. The relief was immense. "Huh," she said, scratching hard and still facing the mountain. "You look different. Bear has bare rock. Bear has bare. Bear is bare. Bare bear."

§

Rise and shine for the maritime. Time for coffee! The mountain had watched so many patterns, of course, and this creature's was pretty predictable. Coffee, stretching, walking, food, work inside or out. Slowing down a bit, over the years. Aging. Shoulders and soul bent. The mountain felt an itch, a very bad itch, and thus did a small shake.

§

Rock had probably saved this cluster of homes. Sleeping Bear Mountain was steep and forested, but near the bottom, where mountain met river, was a run of pure scree. Some of the boulders were the size of cars, but most of it was smaller lichen-covered granite hunks. The wildfire had burned up to the edge of it. Had the flames leaped over it, and to the trees along the riverbed, the houses in this small meadow would have all burned. But it was as if nature had put out a stop sign. Nova was surprised that the rocks were not blackened or dark—no, they sat unchanged, a green-gray tumble. A few smaller ones tumbled down at this very moment, surely falling into the river below, though she couldn't see their landing from where she was at, the river being blocked by trees and a few other houses. The scree reminded her of all the stone in Italy, stacked and lined and used for some purpose. Stone streets, stone walls, stone buildings. She whispered *thanks* to the stone, then sat up, put her feet on floor.

§

What's next for me? The mountain had wondered for a long time. Sure, there were familiar expected regular changes: the chill of heavy snow, the feeling of water sliding over skin as springmelt came, the tickle of new growth as pasque flowers emerged, the heat-beat of summer sun. And the mycelial chitchat, oh, now that was joy! And the kablamies, too: being pushed up 80 million years ago or so, eroded by glaciers, collisions between plates, volcanoes and ash. Frontrangia. Ancestral Rockies. Magma silica, metal oxides, feldspar, quartz. Too much carbon, now. The air was different. The heat was different. So, what next? That was the question! Maybe that great mountain far to the frontside of her would finally erupt, or a meteor would crash, or an earthquake would tear. But likely, the change was going to be in the air. Her next adventure would not be a violent kablamy, it would be a quiet, insidious, secretive one.

§

In all her humanness, Nova had to get up to pee. No more Sleeping Woman for her. Time to rise. And as she did, she thought, *surely, I'll laugh and feel light again here, as in Urbino.* What a seismic shift that trip had been for her. How glad she was that she'd just gone! Surely soon she'd have good times here, too—sit around a campfire with her hippie friends on the mountain, someone with a guitar, all smoking weed—although, no, there would likely not be any campfires in her future. No more fires after this. No one would associate fire with anything fun and light anymore, ever. She'd find something else to signal joy and community. She did love these people, after all—such a mishmash of ages and politics and levels of education and sanity.

But how, she wondered, would they come together? By doing trail work and restoration volunteering? Homebuilding? Mourning ceremonies? She needed to reach out and connect with her peeps once again.

§

If I could choose, the mountain mused, *I suppose I'd like to be under the sea again. Watch fish and octopi and listen to the whales.* But then felt immediately bad, since Mama Home Bear heard. The limping bear scowled and hung her head even lower. *I'm just kidding, Mama Home Bear. I prefer you to starfish.*

Mama Home Bear looked up, eyes dark, and stood on her haunches and scratched an aspen with just one paw, leaving small claw marks on tender bark. *It's all right,* said Mama Home Bear. *I'd like to get off of you and see the ocean, too.*

Mountain laughed, which sent a few more rocks tumbling.

Mama Home Bear huffed with laughter too, but said, *I'm tired. I need to sleep. I need a den for winter and it's late and now they're all—*

—I know, said Mountain. *I'm sorry. But tell ya what, see. If you circle around to my other side, go down the drainage, and over to the Mouse-Ears Mountain, there's a rock outcrop that might suit you, unburned forest all around with a corridor to more. It's new territory for you, I know, but it's still serviceable. There's a small meadow below that survived and in spring there will be aspen catkins and later your elderberry and serviceberry and rosehips.*

The bear fell to all fours, nodding her thanks, and started the journey, looking back at the community she was used to roaming, the one where she'd sought out the occasional bird-feeder or trashcan. Then she lumbered on, stopping once in a while to lick her paw.

§

Nova couldn't wash her hands. She stared at the soap she'd just pumped onto her palms, the sink faucet on but running no water. No duh. The well needed electricity, so she'd packed her car with three-gallon containers filled with water from town. She got her water bottle and poured enough water to get the soap off, then went and lugged the larger container into the bathroom to flush the toilet. Something about dumping water in the back of a toilet to flush made her realize all she'd taken for granted. Made her realize just how much water toilets used. Made her realize just how much humans needed. Of everything. And there were eight billion people like her.

And speaking of water: when the well worked, would the water now be contaminated because of the fire retardant? She'd heard that orange stuff was safe but didn't believe that for a second. Solving one problem by creating another problem seemed to be the way of humankind.

She went to make coffee with her camp stove as if camping in her own home, which felt vaguely confusing. As she waited for the water to boil, she ran her eyes across her backyard. "Heya, Sweet Home," she said, which is what she'd named the double-wide. Though snow was spitting, none was sticking down low here, and so her view was dried grass, cut low by herself before evacuating. It had been green then, as were the cottonwood and aspen, and there had been hummingbirds, who had, of course, now left. The seasons had changed and the mountain had burned, but there was the old silver propane tank, for instance—thank god it hadn't exploded. A magpie flew between her and the mountain. Then a chipmunk ran by. Then a Steller's jay.

She opened her back door and was smacked by an even stronger smell of fire that whooshed in with a blast of cold. A blue sticky note was on her back door. She peeled it off and held it at a far distance to read. YOUR HARD WORK PAID OFF. Tears flushed her eyes. She and the neighbors had worked so hard during that first week, when the fire was only two acres and had just been reported. All that brush clearing, tree cutting, defensible space. Though the scree had protected her on the river side, the fire had also moved down valley, and the fire line had held, she'd heard, because of lack of fuel. Plus, a bit of luck.

She bundled up in a blanket and went outside to drink the coffee. Everything in her fridge had gone bad, and she'd deal with that in a moment, but she still had some oat milk in a cupboard to add because coffee was best when creamy. She missed the little Italian coffees, she missed the smell of Urbino. But while there, she had started to miss here. Now that she was here, she'd miss there. Such was the way of humans.

She was struck by a memory of climbing in the sulfur spring caves of her childhood in Steamboat Springs. Holding her breath against the stench of rotten eggs. Dark and dank and slimy with a blue-green shellacked layer of bubbling something. Adults had told her not to go in, which was fine, because gut instinct told her it was dangerous, too, so she always kept sunlight visible and never knew how deep the caves ran. It was the smell which eventually drove her out because she knew, even as a child, that that was what hell was—being trapped forever in a burning stench.

§

If you look closely now, you'll see Mama Home Bear, who can smell like 2,000 times better than you and is therefore suffering even more because pew-whee, that's rank, isn't it?! Say your goodbyes, mmkay? The mountain hoped the creature's eyes would seek out the black bear, so the two living beings could have a moment of connection. There were things to notice in geologic time and there were things to notice in immediate time, and Mama Home Bear, who was impregnated and leaving the mountain for good, was something worth witnessing. On the other hand, these creatures' eyes seemed to be so bad; it was pitiful, really. Whether seeing a literal bear walking across a mountainside or seeing into the future, their skills seemed to be whoo-eee yikes unhoned.

§

There was a huge pile of bear poop in her yard, Nova saw now. Fresh, too. That made her smile. She'd been told that Home Bear was still around, though now limping, and was renamed Lefty Bear. Everyone wondered: perhaps the bear had burned one foot? Perhaps she'd twisted it while galloping away from flames? And how had she survived, anyway? Just been lucky? Run to safety in the aspen? Gone into the river while the fire flamed around?

She wondered now: did Bear's nose ache from the smell, too?

Then she realized: oh, the bear had no familiar place to go, either!

She and the Home Bear and Sleeping Bear Mountain were all stuck.

Well, so be it. They'd wait out their lives, watch the patterns. It was because nothing mattered that everything mattered, and it did matter that the snow had started to pick up. The world covered in white was a wonderous thing indeed. By the end of the hour, the snow would define the lines that creased Sleeping Bear Mountain, defining her haunch as she rested. Nova was tired herself. Jet lag and all. Aging and all. Trauma and all. Seeing what she'd just seen and all. Maybe she'd head back to bed, despite the coffee.

§

The mountain watched the bear wander in search of a new den, watched the woman in her den bundled in a blanket. *How shivering beautiful that we all watch one another in this blink of time*, the mountain mumbled. *How simple and true: that we witness fires rage* and die, that we look up and notice the moon crossing our viewshed in its various forms, full and half and fingernail. That we sleep to wake, that we rest so we can heal, and that we scramble for survival until our blink is done. What a good blink I'm having! Yesssssireeee, I do appreciate boinking out of the crust of this blue spinning ball at this particular blink in time, whoo-eee, it's a miracle, indeed.

Epilogue:
The fawn in the poppies

THE FAWN WAS BORN IN JUNE, AS FAWNS ARE. BORN DURING the flash floods, which were unprecedented and new. Given that the hardened, black soil could not absorb moisture, the rains next year caused rockslides and mudslides which filled the river with sediment, killing all trout in a ten-mile stretch and killing one human named Bob as dead timber and rocks slushed down a mountainside and into his house as he sat, unawares, likely watching rain hit black mountainside.

But still, the fawn came, and Gretel watched it stand, wobbly-kneed and spotted and wet. *For the love. For the love of all that was holy, a fawn.* It was born over by the lilacs, whose purple flowers were already fading, though the poppies below were not yet in bloom. Gretel could see their fuzzy-green oval heads bending under the weight of the red-orange burst that was about to emerge.

So, the fawn came in the rain. Within its first moments of life, it turned and blinked in the window at Gretel before turning to find mother's milk. Somewhere up-mountain, mulch was being dropped by helicopters and being spread by volunteers, and from that, some weeds were spreading too, given unintended consequences and all. Small trees were being replanted, and the occasional hiking trail had been reopened after crews chain-sawed down the dead trees. There was much healing to be done, and some of it would only happen after nature had taken her own sweet and necessary time.

Norman rolled over and brought Gretel to him. And she brought him to her. But she kept her eyes on the fawn and lilacs and poppies as they made love, an act of defiance against the heartache of the world and in appreciation of the glory. Later, the fawn—curious, or bored, or just because—walked toward the sliding glass door, and since it was becoming increasingly foggy out, pressed its nose onto glass so as to see how all creatures, everywhere and always, dipped their noses into wild-flowers.

—

Acknowledgements

Enormous thanks to my readers: Laura Resau, Karye Cattrell, Todd Mitchell, Claire Boyles, and CMarie Fuhrman. Thanks to my firefighting neighbors Mark Neuroth and Dick Wolfe, who were kind enough to check the details of many of these stories and tell stories of their own. For advising on history and details, thanks to Adam Sowards, Evonne Ellis, Caleb Zurstadt, Aaron Abeyta, Alyson Hagy, and Gabriella Lopez.

I want to thank two towns—the actual unincorporated entitles of Laporte and Bellvue, Colorado. Though I have traveled widely, I have always lived in this general location, and I have always wished to be a fierce see-er of this one spot of Planet Earth. In his introduction to Nan Shepherd's *The Living Mountain*, Robert Macfarlane points out that the word "parochial" now has negative associations—insular and small—but it hasn't always been so. In other meanings of the word, the parish is not a perimeter but an aperture; the parochial is a way of accessing universal truths consisting of "fine-tuned principles, induced from an intense concentration of the particular." By closely observing the external, we can access the most honest internal landscapes of the human experience. That is what I hope to do. So, thank you, towns. Thank you to all the unsung heroes in these towns who took in people and animals, rebuilt homes, joined restoration efforts, and generally supported one another during suffering—as did people across the West and the world. The level of exhaustion was matched by the level of generosity. My place is ecotone—a place at the base of the mountains where several ecosystems merge (in more ways than one); a magical and verdant place with a long history of human occupation, including Arapahoe, Cheyenne, and Ute people, whose continual presence I acknowledge and whose stories I will continue to learn from and whose care of this land will inspire my own.

For their love and true support, I thank my map-making partner, Michael, whose work does the world good, and to Jake and Eliana, my wonderous children, who have grown up in times more traumatic than I would have wished but have somehow found more grace and humor than I could have dreamed. To my students and peers at the Graduate Program in Creative Writing at Western Colorado University for giving me the space and place to develop and direct the Nature Writing MFA program—one of the few in the nation dedicated to responding ethically to our current climate and environmental realities with honesty and compassion.

To Torrey House Press, whose mission overlaps with my own: to be a voice for the land. Amen. Thank you. Kirsten Johanna Allen, Scout Invie, Will Neville-Rehbehn, Gray Buck-Cockayne, and Kathleen Metcalf, you are doing beautiful things. May independent publishers and bookstores thrive with the support of readers everywhere. I also thank the teachers and librarians of my youth and editors at journals and magazines later—so many have helped me become a better reader and writer, a journey that will continue for the rest of my days. Above all else, I thank you, my readers.

This is a work of fiction, though certain stories first birthed themselves as nonfiction and certain events are true. For example, when I was a teenager, my mother really did dig up a skeleton in an old cemetery on the family farm to save it from falling in a ditch during a flood, and I wrote about this as nonfiction for *High Country News*. That said, no characters are based on actual neighbors and I didn't have tents in my yard (the larger community absorbed evacuees) and I do not purport to be an expert on any topic. I know only what I know—and I've done my best to render it by creating fictions of love and joys and sorrows and trauma and healing to tell the urgent truth of wildfire and climate chaos. My ardent hope is that more realistic and imaginative stories take on the subject of our burning planet, and my last acknowledgment goes to all the artists and policymakers and scientists and others who are trying to respond to our reality and our grief and hope. To that end, I offer another quote by Amitov Ghosh from *The Great Derangement*, because this novel and my next, *Three Keys*, were written in response to this: "That climate change casts a much smaller shadow within the landscape of literary fiction than it does even in the public arena is not hard to establish. To see that this is so, we need only to glance through the pages of a few highly regarded literary journals and book reviews…when the subject of climate change occurs in these publications, it is almost always in relation to nonfiction; novels and stories are very rarely to be glimpsed within this horizon…But why? Are the currents of global warming too wild to be navigated in the accustomed barques of narration? But the truth, as is now widely acknowledged, is that we have entered a time when the wild has become the norm: if certain literary forms are unable to negotiate these torrents, then they will have failed—and their failure will have to be counted as an aspect of the broader imaginative and cultural failure that lies at the heart of climate chaos."

The following pieces were originally published in a slightly different form in the following publications:

"Deer in the poppies" appeared in *Ecotone*

"One foot in the black" appeared in *Talking River Review*

"Dirt: A Terra Nova Expedition" is part of a play of the same name that premiered at Bas Bleu Theatre in Fort Collins, Colorado

"Tam's renovation" adapted from an essay in *Creative Nonfiction Magazine*

"Norman's ten seconds in the snow" adapted from an essay in *Terrain*

"Play, hands" adapted from an essay in *The Sun*

"Naomi's Chart of Demise" adapted from the essay "Drag" in *The Sun*

"Our shifting fire" adapted from an essay in *Salon*

"Korine's Acknowledgement of White Owl's Power" adapted from the essay "Door to the Beyond" in *The Colorado Review*

"One, two, three, and a white junker car" adapted from an essay in *The Normal School*

"Feather's eye" adapted from a story in *Tiny Seed Literary Magazine*

"Naomi's calls on the Crisis Hotline" adapted from an essay in *Camas*

"After-Math Ranch" adapted from "Rattlesnake Fire" in *Hell's Bottom, Colorado* (2001), reprinted with permission from Milkweed Editions

Author's Note

This is a work of fiction, though it leans heavily on the reality of the Cameron Peak Fire, Colorado's largest, which burned over 200,000 acres and filled the air with toxic smoke from August to December of 2020. Thousands of people were evacuated and over 500 structures burned. High heat, high winds, and the coronavirus complicated everything. My home sits on one of the evacuation perimeters of that wildfire, and I began writing stories based on that lived experience and my memories of being previously evacuated in 2012, though I want to clarify that the book is ultimately and most honestly expressed as a work of fiction. The details are not intended to be factually accurate. The stories were borne of my imagination in order to access and tell emotional truths.

About the Author

Laura Pritchett is the author of five novels. Her first book, *Hell's Bottom, Colorado*, won the PEN USA Award for Fiction and the Milkweed National Fiction Prize. This was followed by the novels *Sky Bridge, Stars Go Blue, Red Lightning*, and *The Blue Hour*, which garnered other awards including the WILLA, the High Plains Book Award, and the Colorado Book Award. She's also written two nonfiction books, *Great Colorado Bear Stories* and *Making Friends with Death*. Environmental issues are close to her heart, and she's the editor of three anthologies about conservation. She directs the MFA in Nature Writing at Western Colorado University and teaches around the country. She lives in Bellvue, Colorado. www.laurapritchett.com

Torrey House Press

Torrey House Press publishes books at the intersection of the literary arts and environmental advocacy. THP authors explore the diversity of human experiences and relationships with place. THP books create conversations about issues that concern the American West, landscape, literature, and the future of our ever-changing planet, inspiring action toward a more just world.

We believe that lively, contemporary literature is at the cutting edge of social change. We seek to inform, expand, and reshape the dialogue on environmental justice and stewardship for the natural world by elevating literary excellence from diverse voices.

Visit www.torreyhouse.org for reading group discussion guides, author interviews, and more.

As a 501(c)(3) nonprofit publisher, our work is made possible by generous donations from readers like you.

Torrey House Press is supported by Back of Beyond Books, the King's English Bookshop, Maria's Bookshop, the Jeffrey S. & Helen H. Cardon Foundation, the Sam & Diane Stewart Family Foundation, Diana Allison, Karin Anderson, Klaus Bielefeldt, Joe Breddan, Casady Henry, Laurie Hilyer, Frederick Klass, Susan Markley, Kitty Swenson, Shelby Tisdale, Kirtly Parker Jones, Katie Pearce, Molly Swonger, Robert Aagard & Camille Bailey Aagard, Kif Augustine Adams & Stirling Adams, Patti Baynham & Owen Baynham, Rose Chilcoat & Mark Franklin, Jerome Cooney & Laura Storjohann, Linc Cornell & Lois Cornell, Susan Cushman & Charlie Quimby, Kathleen Metcalf & Peter Metcalf, Betsy Gaines Quammen & David Quammen, the Utah Division of Arts & Museums, Utah Humanities, the National Endowment for the Humanities, the National Endowment for the Arts, the Salt Lake City Arts Council, the Utah Governor's Office of Economic Development, and Salt Lake County Zoo, Arts & Parks. Our thanks to individual donors, members, and the Torrey House Press board of directors for their valued support.

Join the Torrey House Press family and give today at www.torreyhouse.org/give.